"It's too late, Lisa,"
he muttered thickly

"Five years too late for apologies. Don't worry, you won't find me any less able than any of your other lovers."

Lisa felt a growing wave of panic. Rorke was going to make love to her! No, not make love to her—punish her. She bit back a shocked cry as his lips moved lingeringly over her skin, caressing the soft swell of her breast. Panic and pain exploded inside her. Her body felt feverish with a need she wasn't going to admit to. She had to get away before Rorke completely overwhelmed her....

She tried to push him away again, gasping out loud when he grasped her wrists, pinning them behind her back, exposing her naked body to the totally male appreciation of his eyes....

Harlequin Presents
by Penny Jordan

These books may be available at your local bookseller.

For a free catalog listing all titles currently available,
send your name and address to:

Harlequin Reader Service
P.O. Box 52040, Phoenix, AZ 85072-9988
Canadian address: Stratford, Ontario N5A 6W2

PENNY JORDAN

forgotten passion

Harlequin Books

TORONTO • NEW YORK • LONDON
AMSTERDAM • PARIS • SYDNEY • HAMBURG
STOCKHOLM • ATHENS • TOKYO • MILAN

Harlequin Presents first edition February 1984
ISBN 0-373-10667-X

Original hardcover edition published in 1983
by Mills & Boon Limited

CHAPTER ONE

LISA was half-way up a pair of step-ladders, trying
to disentangle herself from a piece of wallpaper
that seemed to think its purpose in life was not so
much to decorate the wall but rather to cling
lovingly to her, when she heard the doorbell ring.

Extricating herself with difficulty from its
clinging stickiness, she descended the ladder. She
had worked on too long, she acknowledged,
surveying the almost finished room, and now she
was overtired. Wiping sticky hands on the jeans
she kept on one side for decorating jobs, and
grimacing rather ruefully at their tight shabbiness,
she headed for the door.

She had a good idea that her unexpected caller
would be her new next-door neighbour. When she
had bought her small terraced house in East
London several years ago the area had been
unfashionable and consequently cheap enough to
be within her price range. Fashions changed, and
now the area had been invaded by the new 'with-it'
set, and although their arrival had added a very
healthy sum to the value of her house, Lisa was
beginning to find her new neighbours a little
tedious.

They were both in fashion; Paul seemed to be
away a good deal, and Janice, obviously at
something of a loose end, tended to call round
most evenings on the pretext of wanting to borrow
something, only to stay most of the evening. And

evening was her most productive time of day, Lisa thought wryly. As an illustrator for magazine articles and children's books she found it increasingly difficult to work with the concentration required during the day, mainly because even though Robbie now attended play-school for several hours most days, he was such a lively, intelligent child that Lisa sometimes found it hard going keeping pace with him. Since she needed to work, she had taken to using the evening hours when he was in bed, finding it easier to concentrate when half of her mind was not worrying about the ominous silence which, when combined with an active four-year-old, spelled trouble.

The doorbell pealed again; almost imperiously so, and with another sigh, Lisa closed her bedroom door behind her and headed downstairs.

As she opened the front door on the November darkness and saw the tall, broad-shouldered man standing there with his back to her, her first thought was one of stifled impatience, her automatic reaction to close the door before he could begin whatever sales pitch had brought him to her door. But he moved fast, faster than her, lean brown fingers grasping the door and wrenching it from her. The hall light revealed his face to her and Lisa gasped, stepping backwards instinctively on legs suddenly made of rubber.

'Rorke!' she stammered, eyes widening in shocked disbelief.

'That's right,' he agreed laconically. But there was nothing laconic in the way he was looking at her; in the searing path of his eyes—eyes that were still the same rich turquoise of the seas off St

Martins—as they moved with an insolence she didn't remember over the length of her legs in her too tight jeans, and then upwards, resting blatantly on the curves of her breasts.

Her breath constricted in her throat, the old familiar tension sweeping over her, only now it was more intense; now she had so much more reason to feel tense and afraid in this man's presence.

She pushed a hand into the silky tangle of blonde curls lying on her shoulders, a deeply painful colour suffusing her entire body as he caught the tiny betraying gesture and watched her with eyes as cold and distant as ice.

'Save the coy little tricks for those who appreciate them, Lisa,' he told her brutally. 'I know exactly what it feels like to run my hands through that tempting golden mass, so there's absolutely no need to draw my attention to it.'

It was useless to protest that drawing his attention to her had been the last thing on her mind and that the action had simply been a nervous reflex, something she had done since childhood, as he ought to know.

'What do you want, Rorke?'

The resignation in her voice seemed to please him.

'That's better,' he approved mockingly, 'I want to talk to you, Lisa, and I don't have a lot of time, I've wasted too much already trying to find you.'

'I'm surprised you bothered.' She muttered it under her voice, but it was obvious that he had heard. That was something else she should have remembered, Lisa thought despairingly, wondering bitterly why it was that one glance at this man had been enough to undo five careful years of not thinking about him; of damming up the past and living a life that had started the day her plane touched down at Heathrow and she had left St Martins behind her for ever.

'It wasn't by choice,' Rorke assured her, adding suavely, 'Aren't you going to invite me in? Or do you prefer an audience?'

He glanced to where her neighbour was standing in her bay window, openly appraising him, and suppressing the tiny thread of fear his appearance had reawakened, Lisa turned on her heel, throwing open the living room door.

Like the rest of the house, she had decorated it herself, in soft peaches and coffees; an inexpensive cord carpet covered the floor, and the rest of the furniture could best be described as cheap and cheerful, she knew, but did Rorke have to look at his surroundings so obviously contemptuously?

'Quite a change,' he drawled at last. 'Why, Lisa? Or are you enjoying the sackcloth and ashes bit; the noble penitent paying for her sins?'

Compressing her lips, Lisa refused to be baited. She had lost too many battles to him in the past to be trapped in another one now.

'What do you want, Rorke?' she repeated.

'Not even going to offer me a drink, when I've flown all this way to see you—and tramped halfway round London? I got your address from the bank—at least I thought I had, but you'd moved and they had no forwarding address. And you haven't drawn your allowance once in five years. Why, Lisa?'

'I didn't need it,' she told him, marvelling at the calmness of her voice, the cool composure of her features as she happened to glimpse them in the mirror.

'No, of course, you wouldn't, would you?' he gibed sardonically. 'You've got a lover to support you. Well, he's going to have to do without you for a while, Lisa.'

'What do you mean?' Her heart was thudding painfully against her chest wall, and she recognised the tactical error even as she made it. She should have kept quiet. But now it was too late and Rorke was smiling at her with cruel satisfaction. God, he was really enjoying this; really taking pleasure in seeing her fear and anxiety.

'Oh, don't worry,' he told her softly, watching her with a cold intensity that made her forget everything else, tiny frissons of an awareness she couldn't deny sensitising her body to his proximity. 'You won't be away long. Just as long as it takes Leigh to die!'

Through the swirling darkness, Lisa heard her own shocked 'No!' as she fought off feelings of sickness and pain. Leigh Hayward, who from the very first moment he had married her mother had treated her like his own daughter; who had spoiled and petted her, until she cc... couldn't remember living anywhere but St Martins and anything but Leigh's protective love. Even when her mother died her loss had been softened by Leigh's love. He had flown from the Caribbean to be with her—she had been at school then, sixteen, and anxious to leave, especially after her mother's death. Sensing her loneliness he had given in to her pleas to be allowed to go home with him. England was cold and damp, she had told him, ignoring the fact that she had spent the first six years of her life there.

She was pining for the Caribbean; for the sun, and for his love.

Always indulgent, he had agreed. Now from the vantage point of twenty-two Lisa sighed, closing her eyes against the pain. Dear God—Leigh! She hadn't thought about him in five years, hadn't allowed herself to do so, and now he was dying . . . She glanced up into the shuttered impassive face of the man opposite her. Didn't he feel anything? He had to. After all, Leigh was his father.

'Cut the hysterics,' he told her cruelly. 'Leigh isn't here to see them, and anyway, emotionalism isn't what he needs right now, but it seems he does need you, Lisa. What is it about you?' he mused, his lips curling faintly, the contempt in his eyes unmistakable.

He stood up suddenly, towering above Lisa for all her five foot eight, his skin darkly tanned from the Caribbean sun; his hair sleek and dark. There was Moorish blood somewhere in his ancestry, Leigh had once told her. The family had owned St Martin's since the sixteenth century. It had been given to them by Elizabeth the First, and rumour had it that one of their buccaneering ancestors had taken prisoner the daughter of a rich Moorish trader and had kept her as his own prize.

Certainly Rorke's taut bone structure hinted that the rumour could be right, and Lisa remembered how as a child she had been fascinated by his family history—fascinated by him, so dark and forbiddingly mysterious, at twenty-four to her thirteen so much more adult . . .

'Leigh,' she asked painfully, dragging her mind away from the past, 'what . . .'

'He developed a critical heart condition shortly after you left,' Rorke told her grimly. 'It's gradually grown worse and worse—there's an operation with a fifty-fifty chance of success, but he refused to consider it unless you come back.'

Lisa moistened her lips. Go back? But that was impossible. There was no going back!

'I'm telling you, not asking you, Lisa,' Rorke warned her softly. 'You're coming with me, even if I have to kidnap you.'

'I can't!' Her eyes betrayed her, lifting to the ceiling. Above them was Robbie's room. Robbie who was the reason she could never go back to St Martins. Robbie, who meant the world to her, but whose birth had barred her for ever from her home.

'Can't, or won't? Whichever it is, you're wrong. You're coming back with me.'

Lisa glanced across the room at him, forcing herself to meet the icy scrutiny of his eyes. There was still one card she could play, one knife she could turn, and hurt her though it did not to be able to go to Leigh, she had to protect Robbie.

'If I did come back, Rorke, what would it be as? Your stepsister, or your wife?' For a moment she thought he wasn't going to speak, and then he moved, and she could tell from the snarling curl of his mouth that he was furiously angry.

'My wife! But you were never that, were you, Lisa? Oh, we went through the ceremony all right, but you already belonged to someone else, and marriage to me was just a shield to hide behind, wasn't it?'

'I don't want to talk about it,' Lisa managed shakily, 'and if you don't mind, Rorke, I'd like you to leave. I'd like to be with Leigh, but it really isn't possible.'

'What are you frightened of?' He was really angry now. 'Losing your lover? If that's all that's bothering you I'll make it worth your while ... financially, of course. Physically, I wouldn't touch you if you were the only woman left on earth!'

She lifted her hand instinctively and bit back a gasping protest of pain as Rork's finger curled round her wrist, threatening to crack her bones with the ferocity of his grip.

'Oh no, you don't!' she heard him grate harshly above her. 'Your lover might let you get away with behaviour like that, but I won't!'

She read his intention in his eyes and backed away like a terrified animal, but the wall was behind her, and there was no escape from the bitter hatred in his eyes, or the hard pressure of his arms as they tightened round her, his breath fanning her hair as he fought to control his rage. There was no way he was going to let her go, Lisa knew that, but rather than plead and betray her fear, she lifted her head proudly, her eyes defying him to do his worst.

Her courage only served to increase his anger; Lisa could feel it in the fierce beat of his heart and the tension that emanated from him.

She felt as though her nerves were stretched like steel wire, her breath locking painfully in her throat.

Get it over with, damn you! she screamed silently inwards, knowing that he was deliberately drawing out her punishment. Did he know what it did to her to be so close to him, to be reminded of how innocently she had looked forward to their marriage; had wanted his possession; and how shattered she had been when . . .

His mouth was a mere breath away from hers. Faintness crept through her as she remembered against her will the subtle mastery of those lips. Without her knowing it her own softened and parted, her thick, long eyelashes quivering against her skin—so pale in contrast to his. He made her look ill and anaemic. A curious weightlessness seemed to seize her; she felt her body relaxing, moulding itself to him, sensations she had kept tightly under control for so long stirring hesitantly.

He was looking at her; and Lisa's eyelashes lifted in obedience to that look, heedless of the consequences of what he might read in her eyes.

Rorke looked at her mouth, and Lisa felt herself quiver intensely. Then suddenly she was released and he was stepping away from her, cynicism carved deeply into the tanned features.

'Oh no,' he said slowly, 'I'm not playing substitute for any man. You'll have to do something about controlling your appetites while we're on St Martin's, Lisa, there's no Mike Peters now to appease them with.'

'For the last time, I'm not coming with you,' Lisa said bitterly, her eyes widening betrayingly as she caught the sound she had been dreading ever since his arrival.

'What's that?' Rorke frowned, as Robbie cried for a second time, his face darkening as he obviously recognised the sound. 'You had the child, then?'

'Did you really expect me not to?' demanded Lisa, suddenly courageous now that the moment was upon her. 'I wanted him even if you didn't! And that's why I can't come back with you, Rorke.' She stared provokingly at him. 'Much as I love your father, Robbie's needs come first. I can't leave him here alone.'

He had his back to her, but Lisa saw him stiffen and tensed herself, dreading the outburst of contempt she was sure would follow her disclosure.

'Then you'll just have to bring him with you, won't you,' Rorke said evenly.

Lisa couldn't hide her shock. 'But you said . . . you said you'd never. . . .'

'My father needs you, Lisa,' he interrupted curtly. 'I seem to remember a time when you needed him when your mother died. You owe it to him to be there, Lisa!'

'I can't just leave like that. I need time,' she pleaded.

'I'll give you twenty-four hours,' Rorke announced tautly, preparing to leave. 'And your answer had better be yes! You've a week to get yourselves fixed up with inoculations, etc., and then we'll fly out to St Martin's together.'

Lisa followed him out into the hall, too bemused to question his assumption of authority.

'Oh, and by the way, Lisa,' he paused and turned, the dim light in the hall concealing his expression from her. 'In answer to your earlier question, as my WIFE. You return to St Martins as my wife.'

'And Robbie,' Lisa protested. 'What . . .'

'You are my wife, so it follows that Robbie could be my child, and we'll leave it at that, Lisa. It will please my father if nothing else.'

'But . . .'

'But we both know that can't be so; that you could never have had a child of mine, don't we?' he asked savagely. 'But no one else knows that, do they, Lisa? Even Mike assumed that I had enjoyed my matrimonial rights.' His mouth twisted bitterly. 'I could never understand what spell you'd worked on him. He was your lover and yet he seemed to accept that you'd married me; he even accepted that he didn't have exclusive rights to your favours. How old is . . . is the child?' he demanded suddenly.

'Five, Robbie is nearly five.' Her mouth had gone dry, and she saw from his expression that he had made his own valuation. 'Mike's child, the child you were carrying when you married me!' he said softly, adding savagely, 'God damn you to hell, Lisa,' as he opened the door and walked through it.

Only when he had gone did Lisa move, going automatically upstairs to where Robbie slept in his bed. His little-boy face in sleep had an innocence and purity that tugged at her heart-strings. Mike's child, Rorke had said, and he had flung the words at her like an accusation, but Robbie wasn't Mike's child, he was Rorke's son, although Rorke himself would never believe it, would never even believe that they had been lovers! It was only after he had gone that Lisa realised that Rorke had left his gloves behind. She recoiled from their touch as she picked them up, wishing he had never come back into her life, as she prepared for bed.

She had first realised she loved him when she

was sixteen; the year her mother had died and Leigh had brought her home from England.

She still had a vivid memory of her arrival at St Martin's. They had flown British Airways to St Lucia and from there BIWA to the island, the small inter-island plane dipping low over the azure silk of the Caribbean before landing on what was virtually a levelled-out piece of ground close to the main house.

In those days it had been Leigh and not Rorke who looked after their complicated business interests; including the stake the family held in a chain of luxury hotels dotted through the Caribbean.

On St Martins, though, there was no hotel, only the graceful colonnaded Great House built during the sugar-rich years of the eighteen-hundreds when the family had sent their sons and daughters to London and had thought nothing of commissioning every luxury under the sun to be shipped out to their own small empire.

Leigh's family had been fortunate and wise enough to make good investments, and so, unlike many of their neighbours on the other islands, there was no need for them to sell out.

As she had done the moment she first set foot on the island at the age of six following her mother's marriage to Leigh, Lisa had felt a surge of pleasure as she stepped out of the plane; a feeling of homecoming so intense that for a few seconds it completely obliterated the pain of losing her mother.

Mama Case, who ruled the household with a rod of iron and who had been Leigh's nurse and Rorke's after him, had opened her arms and Lisa had run straight into them. It had been an emotional homecoming. Her mother had been more popular with the native staff than Rorke's French mother, who, so Lisa gathered from them, had never ceased pining for the sophistication of Paris.

It was only later, adult herself and a mother, that Lisa had wondered if Rorke had perhaps resented her mother taking the place of his. If so, he had never betrayed it. Too old to adopt her mother as his own when the marriage took place, he had nevertheless developed a warm and affectionate relationship with her, just as she had with Leigh.

Her own father had died when she was six months old—meningitis, her mother had told her, but Lisa suspected that her mother's love for Leigh was far deeper than the emotion she had felt for her first husband.

In their mutual grief it was only natural that she and Leigh should draw even closer together, but she hadn't realised how much until Mama Case told her gently one evening that they were shutting Rorke out.

'Leigh his daddy too,' she reminded Lisa, 'and that boy sure thought a lot of yor ma, Miss Lisa.'

After that Lisa had made more effort to include Rorke in their conversations, even to the extent of slipping away from the dinner table earlier than usual to give Rorke a chance to talk to his father alone.

She hadn't realised that Rorke had seen through her ploy until he found her on the verandah one evening, swinging in the hammock that her mother had always loved, her face wet with tears.

The day had been a particularly close one. Leigh had been irritable with Rorke over dinner. Lisa had gathered from the conversation that Rorke was keen to modernise several of the hotels and father and son had exchanged heated words.

'You can't live in the past for ever, Father,' he said curtly. 'Nor can you grieve for ever.'

Lisa had left then, sympathising with them both; Leigh whose feelings she understood so well, and Rorke who was so much of an enigma to her, but whose smile had the power to twist her insides with delicious pain, and whose bronzed body did strange things to her pulse rate.

Her very awareness of Rorke was something she was finding it hard to come to terms with. She had always worshipped him, adoring him from a distance, but before it had merely been the innocent admiration of a child. Now there was something different. At school the previous term many of the girls had held giggled conversations about their boy-friends; but Lisa had held slightly aloof, half shocked by their disclosures.

And yet since her return to St Martin's she had found herself becoming aware of Rorke in a way she had not been before, noticing things about him such as the lean hard length of his body as he emerged from the swimming pool where he swam several lengths before breakfast every morning.

The brevity of trunks which previously had gone unnoticed now brought blushing confusion to her cheeks and a desire to avoid his too-seeing eyes.

One half of her was shocked by the wantonness of her thoughts, the other wondered what it would be like to touch the hard maleness of his body, to be kissed by him and touched . . .

'Lisa?'

He moved very quietly for such a big man and she jumped, the swinging seat creaking wildly with the jerkiness of her movement as she turned towards the sound of her name and saw him coming towards her out of the dusk, his white shirt a blur in the darkness slashed by the brown vee of his exposed throat and upper chest.

'Are you okay? Dad thought we might have upset you with our quarrelling.'

His sardonic expression, the way he leaned casually against the verandah, arms folded against his chest, made her ask, 'But you didn't?'

'Not unless you're a far more sensitive plant than the rest of your sex,' he said wryly. 'Besides, you've been coming out here after dinner every evening this last week.'

'I know you like to talk over business matters with your father,' Lisa told him, wishing she could see his expression as clearly as she was sure he could see hers.

This was the longest conversation they had had since her return, apart from the occasion when he had told her of his sorrow at the death of her mother.

'You're a tactful little scrap,' he told her, his voice suddenly disconcertingly warm. 'That's your mother in you, I suppose. What do you plan to do with your life, Lisa?'

It was something she hadn't really thought about, and as though he read her mind, he said hardly, 'You won't be sixteen going on seventeen for ever; there's a whole wide world out there, and if you don't sample at least some of it, you're a fool.'

'You seem quite happy to stay here on St Martins,' Lisa pointed out, not liking the steel in his voice, the hint that she mustn't plan on making her life on St Martins, and like a cold wind chilling her came the realisation that she was nothing really to him, nothing to Leigh who had never legally adopted her although she knew it had always been his intention.

'I'm eleven years older than you and I've seen my share of the world. Besides, I have a purpose here, and my family . . .'

'All right, you don't need to remind me any more that I don't belong here,' Lisa bit out, interrupting him, more angry than she could ever remember being in her life. 'Anyway,' she told him childishly, 'it isn't up to you, it's Leigh who says whether I can stay here or not, and . . .'

'And he's clinging to you because you remind him of your mother,' he told her grimly. 'Is that what you really want from life, Lisa? Out here the living's easy, we all know that, but you're too young for easy living; and if you're not careful it can become degenerative.'

She looked up at him and his mouth twisted wryly. 'What's the matter? Don't you believe me? Take a look around you; look at the native island girls, most of them mothers before they're fifteen. Like I said, life out here is too easy.' He turned and Lisa saw the almost brooding quality of his frown.

Why was Rorke so anxious for her to leave St Martins? Surely he wasn't jealous of her relationship with his father?

'Rorke,' she said his name, huskily and uncertainly, trying to conceal the faint tremor.

'Lisa—Rorke!' Both of them turned at the sound of Leigh's voice, and Lisa decided she must have imagined the look she had glimpsed in Rorke's eyes before his father arrived, because just for an instant it had seemed hotly possessive and bitterly resentful of his father's arrival.

Although she tried to forget them, Rorke's words kept troubling her. She was thinking about them one morning as she walked along the beach dressed in frayed denim shorts, her sandals in her hand, the breeze flattening her thin tee-shirt against the burgeoning curves of her body as she walked across the sand of her favourite bay, just below the house.

'Hello there!' She came to an abrupt halt as a tall, lean-limbed young man suddenly bounded down the beach towards her, fair hair flopping into his eyes, an engaging grin splitting a face still pale enough for him to be an obvious newcomer.

'I'm looking for Mr Geraint—am I heading in the right direction?' he asked cheerfully. 'Mike Peters at your service, by the way, newly arrived and newly qualified doctor of medicine, appointed to your local hospital. Curer of all ills known to man; and surgeon extraordinaire as well,' he announced, sweeping a mock bow and making Lisa laugh with his friendly absurdity.

'I'm just heading back to the house, we can walk there together,' she told him. 'Are you really? The new doctor, I mean. Leigh told me one was arriving, but somehow . . .'

'You pictured an old greybeard, not the dashingly handsome young blade you now see before you,' Mike Peters clowned, grinning.

'Actually, don't tell anyone, will you, but I still find it hard to believe myself. It's been such a long slog to get qualified, I'm still half afraid, someone's going to creep up behind me, filch my certificate and tell me it's all a mistake—hence the flight to St Martins. Wow!' he exclaimed, coming to a standstill as he saw the house for the first time. 'That's really something, Palladian, isn't it?'

Warming to him more and more by the minute, Lisa agreed that it was, and explained a little of the island's history.

They were just crossing the smooth greenness of the lawn, when Rorke suddenly emerged from the house, his forehead creasing in a frown as he looked from Lisa to her companion.

'Rorke, this is Mike, our new doctor,' Lisa introduced, wondering what had made him look so grim.

'Peters,' Rorke acknowledged, betraying that he already knew of Mike's existence. 'Lisa, Dad's been asking for you.'

'Phew—friendly soul, isn't he?' Mike grimaced as Rorke turned on his heel and left them, adding apologetically, 'I'm sorry, I had no right to say that about your brother.'

'Rorke is my stepbrother,' Lisa told him absently, surprised to see comprehension dawning in Mike's eyes and even further confused by his comprehensive: 'So that's the way the land lies! Look, if you can just direct me back to the village . . . I came out for a walk . . .'

'Billy can run you back in the Moke,' Lisa assured him. 'In fact if Dad didn't want to see me I'd come with you myself.'

'No patients to look after, Peters?' Neither of

them had heard Rorke approach, and his clipped voice and hostile expression puzzled Lisa. What on earth was the matter with him?

Ten minutes later when Mike had left with Billy in the Moke she tackled him about it.

'What on earth was wrong with you, Rorke?' she demanded crossly, 'Poor Mike was so embarrassed!'

'So it's Mike now, is it?' Rorke responded savagely. 'God, Lisa, what is it with you? Haven't they warned you at that damned school of yours about being too forthcoming with strangers?'

'You mean when they ask me to go for a ride in their car and offer me sweeties?' Lisa demanded angrily. 'Rorke, I'm sixteen, not six, and besides, it was obvious that Mike . . .'

'What? Come on, Lisa,' he jeered, 'tell me that Peters is impervious to physical desire, if you dare—it was written all over his face that he wanted you—and no wonder! Dressed like that you're offering an open invitation to rape!'

She wasn't going to cry; she wasn't going to give Rorke the satisfaction! There was nothing wrong with her tee-shirt and cut-off shorts; she had worn them for the last couple of holidays; they were clean and comfortable. What was the matter with Rorke?

'That's a horrid thing to say!' she flung at him. 'And Mike wouldn't do a thing like that. All we were doing was talking; he didn't even try to kiss me!'

'He didn't? Then perhaps it's damned well time that someone did,' Rorke muttered half under his breath, reaching for her, with hands that wouldn't allow any escape, lean tanned fingers biting into her skin as she was hauled against the taut muscularity of his chest, the bronzed flesh rising and falling with the irregularity of his breathing.

'Damn you, Lisa,' he groaned against her hair. 'Why the hell did my father have to go and complicate things by bringing you back here?'

Lisa wanted to protest, to demand that he release her, but a strange weakness was spreading through her veins, a pulsing excitement firing her blood; a wantonness she had never known she possessed urging her to reach up and touch the bronzed flesh exposed by the vee of Rorke's shirt.

'Lisa!' Rorke bit out her name as though he hated her, the sudden pressure of his mouth on hers shockingly intimate, robbing her of breath. 'Open your mouth,' he muttered huskily against her skin, and as though she were completely lacking in any willpower, Lisa felt her lips parting moistly to the sensual intrusion of his. A fierce, painful urge to mould her body against Rorke's rippled through her, shocking her with its mindless intensity. She pulled away, and Rorke released her immediately, allowing her to turn and run into the cool shadows of the verandah.

What on earth had possessed him? What had possessed her? Lisa asked herself fiercely. They were practically brother and sister; or were they?

Shivering despite the tropical heat, she allowed her fingers to touch the sensitive flesh Rorke's mouth had just ravaged. For a moment in his arms she had been oblivious to everything but the strange pulsating need to lose herself in him, to be part of him to ... With a small cry Lisa clapped her hands over her ears, not wanting to listen to the inner voice telling her that she had wanted

Rorke to make love to her. Rorke, who had never shown her anything but careless affection; Rorke who she knew from her mother had a whole contingent of girl-friends; who was worldly and experienced and would surely break her heart if she was ever foolish enough to let him know how easily it had slipped into his possession.

CHAPTER TWO

'THAT young Peters fellow's been on the phone again.' Leigh teased Lisa, several days later after dinner. 'Something about wanting to take you sailing.'

'Lisa isn't going sailing with Peters or any other young fool who thinks because the Caribbean looks placid and blue that it's easy to sail,' Rorke snapped before Lisa could reply.

'Rorke's right,' Leigh palliated, seeing the anger sparkling in her eyes. 'These waters can be dangerous, Lisa. If you're desperate to go sailing why don't you let Rorke take you? You were talking about going over to St Lucia anyway, weren't you?'

'It wasn't the kind of journey where I'd want company, though,' Rorke announced grittily. 'At least not Lisa's. I'd planned to pick up Helen Dunbar.'

Helen Dunbar! A vicelike pain gripped Lisa's heart. Helen Dunbar was one of Rorke's more long-standing girl-friends. A passionate redhead who lived on St Lucia, she had visited St Martins several years previously. Her uncle was Leigh's lawyer and she owned a very exclusive boutique on the other island. Lisa knew that there had been a time when Leigh had worried that their relationship might become more permanent. Leigh had never made any secret of the fact that he wanted to see his son married, preferably with children, but he was old-fashioned enough not to want to see Rorke married to a woman like Helen, to whom Rorke was one in a long line of lovers.

'Who says I'd want to go with you anyway?' Lisa threw back at him. 'You've been like a bear with a sore head recently—ever since I came back, in fact!'

'So you've noticed,' Rorke mocked sardonically, ignoring his father's frown and Lisa's growing anger. 'Full marks, little girl.' He got up as he spoke, pushing away his chair. 'I've got to go and ring the hotel on St. Lucia,' he told his father.

'Don't take any notice of Rorke,' Leigh told Lisa quietly when Rorke had gone. 'I don't know what's got into him recently.'

'He's been really unkind to poor Mike,' Lisa told him, trying not to remember the treacherous feelings she had experienced in Rorke's arms—she couldn't possibly be in love with him, she had told herself; she was too young to fall in love, and not with Rorke of all people!

'Has he?' Leigh frowned. 'In what way?'

'Oh, he told me off because I'd been walking on the beach with Mike. In fact he more or less accused him of being a potential rapist,' Lisa told him indignantly. 'I . . .'

Her cheeks coloured as memories of the hard pressure of Rorke's mouth against hers surged over her, but fortunately Leigh wasn't looking at her. In fact, he looked totally engrossed in his own thoughts.

'Umm,' he said at last. 'Well, despite what Rorke says, I think it might be a good idea if you went to St Lucia with him. It's time you had some new clothes, for one thing.' He glanced at her shorts and tee-shirt, and Lisa grimaced.

'Yes, I know these are indecent—Rorke's already told me.'

'Has he now! Indecent wasn't exactly the word I had in my mind—but you'll certainly need some extra lightweight things. Mama Case tells me you're not a little girl any longer, Lisa, and looking at you now I know that's true.'

'It seems a waste to buy me summer things, when Rorke wants you to send me back to England,' Lisa murmured, voicing the concern that had lain at the back of her mind ever since Rorke had taxed her with it.

'My darling child!' Leigh stood up, placing his hands on her shoulders, his face grave. 'I'm still master on St Martins, and there's simply no way I'm going to allow you to leave. Ignore Rorke, he has his own problems.' A faint smile tugged at the corners of his mouth. 'You'll go to St Lucia with him and buy yourself some pretty clothes—Rorke often has to visit our hotels, and when he does, I think it might be a good idea if you went with him. You're growing up, Lisa, you'll be seventeen shortly. It's time you started taking your place in the adult world.'

An exciting prospect, but somehow Lisa couldn't see Rorke agreeing with it. Ever since he had kissed her, things had been different between them. He had kissed her as some form of punishment, she knew that, but the punishment had been far more bitter than he could know, because it had opened her eyes to so much she had never known existed before when she had thought of 'love' as a rosy, uncomplicated dream. Now she knew better.

Lisa had been playing tennis with Mike—a hot

energetic game which they had drawn. It had been Mike's morning off and now he had returned to the small cottage hospital, and Lisa was going upstairs to shower and rest in her room until dinner.

Leigh was visiting a friend—the family lawyer, who lived on the other side of the island. The two men enjoyed playing chess, and as she revelled in the cool hiss of the shower over her heated skin, Lisa reflected on Leigh's announcement the previous evening that Rorke had agreed to take her with him to St Lucia. Exactly what pressure he had brought to bear on his son to effect his capitulation Lisa couldn't guess, but that Rorke wasn't pleased about the idea had been evident.

Rorke. Her eyes became dreamy, the brisk rubbing she had been giving her skin with her sponge suddenly forgotten as the movement of her hand stilled, quickfire excitement running through her veins. Rorke! His name escaped her lips on a soft sigh, and she had rinsed the suds off her skin before she realised that she had left her towelling robe on her bed. Her feet left damp footprints on the cool tiles of the bedroom floor as she padded across it. Her hand was on the robe when she heard the rattle of someone opening her bedroom door.

'Lisa!' She froze as she heard Rorke's curt voice, too shocked to cry out a warning to him, and then he was in the room with her, his eyes moving in darkening comprehension over the lithe curves of her body still beaded with moisture. Just for a moment time seemed to stand still, as Rorke's gaze skimmed the firm upthrust of her breasts, moving

downwards over her slender waist and long coltish
legs.

And then, as suddenly as he had come in, he
was gone, leaving her to breathe more easily,
shivers suddenly coursing over her heated flesh,
her fingers numb with a panic that came much,
much too late as she pulled on the protective
covering of her robe. Her hand brushed the curve
of her breast, her heart pounding unsteadily. What
was happening to her? She felt as though suddenly
she had a fever, her pulses racing, her body shivery
and aching. Was this what love felt like?

She was very subdued over dinner, hardly able
to bring herself to look at Rorke. Were those brief
seconds imprinted as vividly on his mind as they
were on hers? Of course not, she mocked herself.
She was far from being the first naked woman he
had seen; to him she was simply a schoolgirl still.

'Have you told Lisa you're leaving in the
morning?' Leigh asked Rorke during dinner.

'Not yet. Can you be ready by then?' Rorke
asked her, without looking at her, and as though
he had said the words out loud Lisa knew that he
didn't want to look at her.

'Of course she can,' Leigh announced genially
before she could speak. 'And don't forget, Lisa,'
he added, giving her a warm smile, 'get yourself
plenty of pretty things while you're in St Lucia.

'How long are you planning on staying?' he
asked his son, and again Lisa was aware of
Rorke's deliberate exclusion of her as he shrugged
powerfully.

'A couple of days—no longer. It depends on
how quickly Helen is ready to leave.'

Helen! A pain like red-hot knives bit into her

skin, and it was all she could do not to cry out loud. So this was jealousy; this searing, tearing agony destroying her.

Once again Rorke excused himself the moment the meal was over. Some of Lisa's dismay must have shown in her face, because she realised that Leigh was watching her with some concern.

'Don't worry about Rorke,' he told her gruffly. 'He's going through a difficult time at the moment. I remember when I first met your mother . . .'

Lisa stared at him. What did he mean? Surely Rorke wasn't planning to *marry* Helen? She reminded herself that it was no business of hers if he was, and then wondered why she was weak enough to allow herself to be persuaded into going with Rorke when all the trip to St Lucia was likely to bring her was the pain of seeing him with Helen.

But of course, she couldn't disappoint Leigh, and she knew he *would* be disappointed and hurt if she refused to go. She glanced down at her skimpy cotton dress and suppressed a grimace. Her clothes were getting shabby. Strange how all at once she had become aware of it, mentally comparing herself to Helen, seeing herself with the sophisticated eyes of a man used to elegance and sensuality in a woman.

Mama Case fussed round her at breakfast, complaining under her breath until Rorke said sardonically, 'She'll be safe enough, Mama Case—we're leaving Dr Peters behind!'

Lisa's cheeks stung at the implied suggestion, but somehow she managed to repress the hot words clamouring for utterance. Why should Rorke disapprove of Mike so much? *She* enjoyed

his company. They were on the same wavelength,
he was kind and friendly, his manner very
evocative of that of her friends' brothers towards
her. It came to her with a sudden sense of shock
that Mike was more like a brother to her than
Rorke. Her feelings for Rorke had never been
sisterly, she acknowledged on a sudden wave of
self-awareness; there had always been beneath the
surface a fine thread of tension making it
impossible for her to relax in his company the way
she could with Mike.

'Daydreaming about Peters?'

She came to with a start, realising that Rorke
was propped up against the wall watching her, and
her face coloured again as she worried about what
he might have read in her expression.

'And if I was?' she challenged, tilting her chin,
determined not to allow him to guess that *he* had
been the subject of her thoughts.

'Forget it,' Rorke warned her grimly. 'He might
be a young girl's dream, Lisa, but you won't be a
young girl for ever. One day you're going to be a
woman, and when you are,' he said softly, 'you're
going to want a man, not a boy.'

He was gone before she could retort; before she
could demand that he explain what he meant.

Half an hour later, she was waiting for Leon to
row her out to where Rorke's schooner lay
anchored in the bay below the house. He had
bought it three years earlier, and Lisa had watched
adoringly while he lovingly restored what had
originally been no more than a shell. Now the
graceful vessel swung lazily at anchor, sails furled,
paintwork gleaming. Lisa had been aboard her
several times during her visits home, and was

completely at home on the elegant craft. Leigh himself had taught her to sail, and on one never-to-be-forgotten occasion Rorke had actually allowed her to crew for him when he raced the schooner in a local regatta.

'You can take the for'ard bunk,' Rorke told her grittily, bending to grip her wrist and help her on board. 'Leon's already stowed your stuff. Not that there was much.'

For a moment the brilliance of the sun on the white paintwork dazzled Lisa, and then her vision cleared and she became aware of Rorke standing barefoot on the deck, his denim shorts almost as disreputable as her own, the rest of his body burned a warm teak by the sun and salt.

'Leigh wants me to get some new clothes while we're in St Lucia,' Lisa reminded him, frowning a little as she glanced down at her bare legs and frayed shorts.

'So he told me,' Rorke agreed. 'He seems to think Helen might take you in hand. Quite a challenge, I should think,' he said insultingly, adding, 'I'm going on deck to cast off.'

'Want any help?' Lisa called after him, trying to swallow her hurt, but he barely paused in the narrow doorway to her cabin.

'No, thanks,' he told her curtly. 'I can handle *Lady* on my own—in fact sometimes it's easier that way.'

'Meaning you want me to stay in my cabin until we reach St Lucia?' Lisa demanded, disappointment and pain suddenly overwhelming caution. 'Is that what you're trying to say, Rorke?'

'It might make things easier all round,' he agreed, apparently unaware of the pain he was causing her.

The morning passed slowly for Lisa, cooped up in the small cabin, watching the waves through the porthole and mentally chafing at her imprisonment.

By lunchtime she decided that nothing, but nothing was going to keep her in her cabin any longer. She had originally decided that Rorke would have to get down on his knees and beg her before she would so much as put one foot on the deck, but boredom and hunger had overcome her resolution. Even Rorke had to eat, she reminded herself, and he could hardly do that and sail the schooner as well.

Her rubber-soled sneakers made no sound on the seasoned timbers of the deck as she went in search of Rorke to ask him what he wanted for lunch, but there was no sign of him, and she realised that the schooner was rocking gently at anchor. Where was he?

Tiny shivers of apprehension shuddered down her spine. Surely it was stupid to imagine that an experienced sailor like Rorke could fall overboard in a calm sea? Of course it was. He was probably resting himself! She was just on the point of going down to his cabin to check and had turned away from the deck when a shadow fell across her path.

'Rorke!' She swung round, relief in her voice, and saw Rorke straightening up on the deck, his skin sleek and damp, his hair plastered to his skull, and shock coursed through her, rooting her to the spot as she realised that he was naked, his body glistening tautly brown under the salt water spray.

'Lisa!' She saw his teeth snap together in anger. 'I thought you were going to stay in your cabin?'

'I came to see if you wanted any lunch.'

She had to drag her eyes away from the male perfection of his body, shocking in its masculinity and yet, at the same time, undoubtedly exciting. Tremors of reaction were pulsing through her own skin, a cramping delirium in the pit of her stomach.

'Later, when I've showered and changed. What's the matter?' he demanded tautly when she didn't move, adding impatiently, 'For God's sake, Lisa, get below, before I do something that will really shock you!'

They made St Lucia earlier than Lisa had anticipated, and she had a shrewd suspicion that Rorke had deliberately cut the journey short.

Castries, the main harbour, was busy. A cruise ship had come into port and the town's narrow streets were thronged with trippers. Lisa was forced to fall behind as Rorke's long legs propelled him swiftly through the crowd. At one busy intersection he waited for her to catch up with him, grimacing as he took her arm. His fingers were rough against her skin, and she could see the faint salt bloom on his chest and throat. A wave of faintness came over her as she remembered seeing him step on to the deck after his swim. That it wasn't the first time he had swum nude had been very evident in the depth and extent of his tan, and the faintness increased tormentingly as she wondered if, on those occasions, he had always swum alone, or if, perhaps, someone had joined him—Helen, for instance.

Just for a moment she allowed herself to imagine what it would be like to float motionless beside him in the blue-green depths of the Caribbean, the silky water her only covering.

'Lisa!'

The harshness of his voice jerked her out of her pleasurable daydream and back into the present. They were standing outside Helen's exclusive boutique. Inside both Helen and her assistant were busy serving the cruise liner's passengers, but Helen had obviously seen them.

'We'll go on to the hotel and come back later,' Rorke announced. 'I've warned them to expect us.'

A taxi took them from Castries to the Paradise Cove hotel, in which the family had shares. The hotel was a modern one; a complex rather than a hotel, with chalets spread out through luxuriant grounds and a central hotel block comprising restaurants, bars, half a dozen shops, and a large games room.

They were greeted enthusiastically by the manager, who was obviously anxious to impress Rorke with the smooth running of the hotel, and certainly there was no fault to be found with the speed with which their baggage was taken care of, and complimentary drinks brought to them in the foyer-cum-lounge. While the two men talked, Lisa got up and strolled over to glance at the small parade of shops. One window had an exquisite display of beach and resort wear, another expensive and exclusive casuals. Lisa glanced over her shoulder. Rorke was still deep in conversation with the hotel manager. On a small spurt of rebellion she opened the door to the boutique. She knew Rorke had intended to hand her over to Helen and leave it to the older woman to choose her new clothes, but during her time in England Lisa had often visited the homes of her friends, and had gone with them on shopping expeditions.

She had a natural sense of taste and flair, her mother had always said, and her initial qualms were quickly stifled as a charming and pleasant girl stepped forward to help her.

Quickly explaining what she wanted, Lisa watched the girl riffle through the packed racks of clothes, unerringly selecting half a dozen or so outfits which she piled on to a chair.

'You're lucky,' she told Lisa, as she handed them to her. 'We've only this week received this lot—Jane, my partner, ordered them the last time she went to America—I promise you they're the very latest thing—and quite exclusive.'

They were lovely, Lisa admitted, alone in the cubicle, running her fingers over the fine silks and cottons. A Benny Ong two-piece in vibrant blue and emerald silk caught her eye, and she quickly pulled off her own clothes and slipped the slender sheath of a dress over her shoulders. The colours brought out the deep blue-green depths of her eyes, and the soft golden glints of her hair. The dress was supported by tiny shoestring straps and over it there was a thin matching silk jacket that tied softly in a knot. Looking at her reflection in the mirror, Lisa was astounded at the transformation. The outfit might have been made for her—a verdict fully endorsed by the salesgirl as she came to see how she was getting on.

'It's definitely you,' she pronounced. 'But don't commit yourself until you've tried the others.'

Taking her advice, Lisa tried on everything she brought, and when she eventually emerged from the boutique she had bought the Benny Ong outfit plus an attractive range of cotton separates that she could mix and match for maximum effect;

some brilliant magenta cut-off jeans, and a French bikini so brief that she had blushed to see herself in it, until the salesgirl had assured her that it was absolutely stunning.

There had still been quite a lot left from the money Leigh had given her, so on the salesgirl's advice she had purchased some new underwear—feminine Italian satin and lace that she was sure she would never wear, but which felt so pleasurable against her skin that she hadn't been able to resist it.

Rorke was waiting outside as she opened the boutique door, glowering at his watch.

'What the hell do you think you're doing?' he pounced when he saw her.

'Shopping,' she told him, proud of her calm voice. 'Leigh told me to.'

'I was going to take you to see Helen.'

'I'm perfectly capable of buying clothes for myself without the advice of your mistress,' Lisa told him rashly.

'I hope you're right,' Rorke threatened, 'because we're dining here tonight with Helen and some friends of ours. Helen and Sandra are both very elegant women.'

'In that case I'd better make an appointment to have my hair done,' Lisa told him with commendable aplomb. 'I don't want to let you down.'

'I'll get someone to take you up to your room,' Rorke told her without responding. 'I'm going to see Helen.'

If only her hand wasn't shaking so much, Lisa thought, tongue protruding slightly between her lips as she applied the eyeshadow she had bought on the advice of the girl in the beauty salon. Her hair lay softly sleek against her shoulders, the unruly curls tamed; the herbal rinse the hairdresser used gave off a delicate fragrance that perfumed the air. If Rorke thought she wouldn't compare favourably with Helen and her friend he was going to be proved wrong!

In addition to having her hair done and getting the advice of the girl in the beauty salon Lisa had found time to buy a pair of sandals, striped in emerald and blue leather to tone with her dress.

At last she was ready. She peered anxiously at her reflection. Had she blended the eyeshadow enough? She didn't want to look like a clown! A glimpse in the mirror reassured her. Her own face stared back at her, familiar but subtly different. Her eyes looked larger and darker, the careful blending of blue and green eyeshadow adding a hint of depth and mystery. A coat of mascara added thickness to the luxuriance of her dark lashes, and the coral lipstick she had carefully painted on emphasised the full lower curve of her mouth and the honey translucence of healthy young skin.

She was ready when Rorke tapped on her door, strangely unfamiliar in formal evening clothes, and her heart thumped unevenly as she stared up at him, wondering how on earth she had managed in the past to miss the overt sexuality he exuded.

'Ready?'

His glance swept her dismissively, and Lisa felt anger burn up inside her at his indifference. Surely he must see how different she looked? Why, she even felt different, but he was still treating her as the same little girl who had tagged after him in the past.

Helen and her friends were already in the bar waiting for them, Helen elegant and sophisticated in a white sheath dress that privately Lisa thought a shade too revealing, her elongated cat-like eyes skimming with barely suppressed hostility over Lisa's silk clad figure as she cooed, 'Poor Rorke has to babysit this trip. Leigh insisted that he bring Lisa with him. Never mind, darling,' she comforted Rorke, 'there's always later.'

'You mustn't mind Helen,' Sandra Wilkes murmured understandingly to Lisa as Rorke signalled a waiter. 'She's always been a mite possessive where Rorke's concerned.'

'You certainly don't look much like a baby to me!' Peter Wilkes added with heavy gallantry, giving her an admiring glance. The Wilkes were in their early thirties and seemed a pleasant enough couple. They had two children, Sandra told Lisa over dinner, both at school in England.

'I miss them dreadfully,' she confided, 'but needs must, I'm afraid. Still, Peter's hoping to get a London posting soon, so we should all be reunited. Tell me about the island,' she encouraged. 'According to Helen it's virtually the back of beyond, although I must say it sounds so exciting—one's own island!'

'It's been in Rorke's family for generations,' Lisa told her, 'and I can't see him ever parting with it.'

'He will if Helen has anything to do with it,' Sandra laughed. 'She's told me she's aching to get back to London.'

'I don't think Rorke would agree to that. He'd

want his children to grow up on the island as he did,' Lisa told her, surprised when Sandra's eyes widened. 'Have I said something wrong?' she asked uncertainly.

'Not exactly—it's just that Helen can't have children—can't, and wouldn't anyway—she loathes them.'

'But Rorke . . .'

'Will want a son to come after him?' Sandra supplied. 'Yes, I got that impression too. Still, it's their business, not ours. Personally I've always thought of Helen more as a mistress than a wife. Perhaps Rorke will come to think so too. He could find a dutiful little wife to bear his sons, and still have his fun with Helen.'

'Oh no, surely not!' Lisa protested, thoroughly revolted by the picture Sandra was drawing.

The older woman laughed. 'You're such a baby,' she teased, 'but then how old are you?'

'Seventeen—almost,' Lisa told her.

'Is that all? I thought you were nineteen at least.'

Lisa found her words wonderfully uplifting after Rorke's apparent unawareness of the change in her appearance, but it was hard not to notice how Helen constantly touched Rorke's arm when she spoke to him; their low-voiced murmurs wafting across the table, making Lisa long to get up from the table and run as far and as fast as she could to escape the evidence of their intimacy.

After dinner Helen insisted that she wanted to dance. She knew of a nightclub, she told Rorke. They could all go on there. All except Lisa, she suggested, glancing pointedly at the younger girl.

'Oh, of course she can come with us,' Sandra

protested. 'If she wants to, and I'm sure she does. A pretty girl wearing a new dress always wants to show it off.'

Helen looked far from pleased, and Lisa held her breath, half expecting Rorke to tell her that she was to go to her room, but to her surprise he said nothing, merely looking grimly unforthcoming as Peter took her arm and escorted her from the table.

The nightclub was hot and cramped, and although she wasn't going to admit it, Lisa would have much preferred to be walking along the beach at St Martin's, the soft evening breeze cooling her overheated skin and blowing freely in her hair.

'Lisa?'

She came out of her reverie to find Rorke towering over her while Helen glowered furiously, and Sandra and Peter exchanged comprehensive glances.

'Lisa, I'm asking you to dance,' Rorke reminded her.

'To dance?' She looked up at him wildly, heady excitement racing through her veins. Like someone in a dream she followed him on to the small crowded floor. The steel band were playing a tune with a powerfully sensual beat, and Lisa found her body seemed to have its own rhythm, as Rorke took her in his arms, his palms flat against the bare skin of her shoulders.

'I don't think Helen likes you dancing with me,' Lisa murmured as she glanced towards their table and saw Helen watching them, fury in the catlike eyes.

'Damn Helen,' Rorke muttered ruthlessly,

stunning her with the fierce intensity of his words, his fingers tightening on her shoulders as he drew her closer towards him. 'And damn you, Lisa,' he muttered thickly, 'for making me feel like this. God, you're a child . . . or so I keep telling myself, but seeing you tonight, holding you in my arms . . .'

A tremor ripped through him, and Lisa could see the sheen of perspiration on his face. Rorke— Rorke whom she had always thought of as invincible, was trembling because he was holding her in his arms. She could hardly believe it, but it was true!

'Lisa!' He groaned her name against her hair, holding her even closer, close enough for her to feel the fixed rigidity of his body, the pulsating heat it radiated. His mouth left her hair, seeking the tender curve of her throat. A maelstrom of emotion gripped her. Her body shivered delicately as his mouth plundered the soft sweetness of her skin. His hands shaped her to him, her breasts crushed against his chest, the hardness of his body compelling hers to yield and mould itself to him.

Distantly she was aware of Helen, glaring furiously at her, knowing that she was warning Lisa that she would make her pay for the pleasure of being in Rorke's arms, but she felt too deliriously happy to care. Even so, it wasn't pleasant, feeling Helen's eyes boring into the back of her neck, and as though he sensed her distress Rorke questioned frowningly, 'Is something wrong?'

'It's just that it's so hot in here,' Lisa told him, not wanting to admit that Helen made her feel uncomfortable. What was between them was too new and precious for her to talk freely. She had no idea what had brought about the transformation in Rorke, but she wasn't going to jeopardise it by criticising Helen to him.

'Feel like a walk, then, to cool off?'

There was a disturbing glint in his eyes, a curve to his mouth that made Lisa's heart race.

'That would be very nice,' she managed sedately, hoping he wouldn't guess how understated her comment was.

CHAPTER THREE

'I DIDN'T want to bring you to St Lucia with me.'

'I know.'

They were walking hand in hand along the soft white sand, the moon and the stars their only witnesses. The soft breeze Lisa had longed for in the stifling heat of the nightclub wafted balmily over them. Rorke paused, slipping off his jacket, which he dropped on to the sand. 'Sit down for a moment,' he suggested, adding huskily, 'God, Lisa, have you any idea what you do to me? Any idea of the jealousy I've endured watching you with young Peters?'

'You jealous?' Her voice sounded breathless.

'I'm only human, Lisa,' Rorke reminded her drily. 'All too human where you're concerned.'

'But you've been so unkind to me . . .'

'Not half as unkind as I've been to myself. You're seventeen,' he told her softly, cupping her face. 'A little girl still in so many ways, and yet already a very desirable young woman. I tried reminding myself that you were my stepsister, but it made no difference. The last time you came home I wanted you, Lisa,' he told her bluntly. 'That was six months ago, and nothing has changed, except that I now want you twice as much,' he told her hoarsely. 'So much . . .'

Her whole body quivered in mute response, eager fingers trembling against his skin as she reached towards him.

'Lisa,' Rorke groaned grasping her fingers, and pressing a kiss against her palm. 'I shouldn't be doing this; shouldn't be giving way to what I feel, but God help me, I can't stop myself . . .'

'And I don't want you to,' Lisa told him shyly. 'I love you, Rorke.'

'I thought you loved young Peters,' he mocked sardonically. 'How can you love me when every time I look at you you run away? What do you know of love, Lisa? Until you saw me today I don't believe you'd ever seen a naked man before, never mind . . .'

Hot colour stained her cheeks, but she still found the courage to say hesitantly, 'Does it matter so much, Rorke—that I'm not experienced, I mean? Can't you teach me?'

'Lisa!'

Her name was torn from his throat on an aching protest, and then she was in his arms, his mouth against her skin, tasting, exploring, his lips moving sensuously against hers, parting their soft innocence and probing the sweetness beyond until she was aware of nothing apart from the taste and feel of him as he lowered her to the sand, his hands exploring the contours of her body, his muffled gasp when he suddenly drew away from her confusing her as much as his abrupt withdrawal.

'Leigh at least will be pleased,' he murmured as he pulled her to her feet. 'Surely you've realised how keen he's been to throw us together?' he prodded when Lisa made no response. 'Dear God, you *are* an innocent, aren't you,' he muttered, and despite the warmth of his arm round her body, Lisa felt a strangely apprehensive chill strike through her body. It was almost as though Rorke resented wanting her, resented loving her.

'Rorke?'

As though he sensed her uncertainty his arm tightened.

'Rorke, do you love me?' she murmured softly.

For a moment she sensed his withdrawal and then he was saying smoothly, 'Of course I love you, Lisa, who wouldn't—but right now I think it's time you were back in your virginal bed, don't you?

She wanted to tell him that she would far rather spend the night in his arms, in his bed, but somehow she couldn't find the words. Indeed she was surprised that he hadn't suggested it himself, If she had been Helen! But she wasn't Helen, she reminded herself. She was herself, and Rorke loved her, and surely once they returned to St Martin's and he had told his father, they would be married?

They started the return journey to St Martin's, earlier than had been planned. There was a storm warning, Rorke explained to Lisa when she joined him for breakfast, feeling shyly selfconscious in some of her new separates, and he wanted to get under way as quickly as possible.

'You're not sorry—about what happened last night, are you?' she asked hesitantly.

'Not half as sorry as I am about what didn't,' Rorke responded sardonically. 'Lisa, do you have the faintest idea of what you're letting yourself in for? You're barely seventeen—you haven't even begun to taste life.'

'Rorke, I love you!'

'So you keep telling me, and I'm selfish enough to want to believe it. I ought to send you away, for two years at least, but I can't risk losing you. I love you too much.'

'What do you think Leigh will say?'

'Well, let's put it this way,' Rorke retorted wryly. 'I don't think it's going to come as a complete surprise. Something tells me he's already guessed how I feel about you. In fact I wouldn't put it past him to have engineered this trip with a view to flinging us together. He's been at great pains to point out to me how quickly you're growing up—Growing up! Dear God, and to think I once thought it was only old men in their dotage who found pubescent children physically desirable!'

'I'm not a child,' Lisa protested, hating the cynicism in his eyes and voice. 'In another month I'll be seventeen—another year and . . .'

'And you'll be eighteen—I can count, Lisa. Come on,' he said abruptly. 'Get your things together and I'll check us out. If we leave now we should make it back to St Martins before the weather breaks.'

They left Castries harbour an hour later. The sky was completely free of cloud, but there was a certain dull brassiness about the sun that made Lisa conscious that the storm forecast could not be lightly ignored.

This time there was no question of her staying below. Like Rorke she had changed into her frayed denim shorts, and her body pulsated with excitement as his eyes narrowed over the curves of her breasts, outlined by the stretchy fabric of her tee shirt, as he helped her aboard.

'We'd better use full sail and the auxiliary engine,' Rorke announced laconically once they were both on board. 'I don't like the colour of that sky.'

They had completed just over a quarter of their journey, and Rorke was busy checking their progress in the wheelhouse when he suddenly called to Lisa.

'Damn, we're getting so much interference I can't do a thing with the radio. These electric storms play havoc with the equipment.' The wind had started to pick up and Lisa was relieved when he came back to join her, checking on the sails, frowning occasionally as the schooner started to pick up speed.

'Hell!' he swore softly. 'By the looks of it we're heading right for the storm. It must have changed course. I wish to God we could get some decent radio signals.

'Go below and put on a lifejacket, will you, Lisa,' he instructed curtly, 'and bring one up for me. Don't look like that,' he added when he saw the concern in her eyes. 'I'm just taking precautions.'

'How bad is it going to be, Rorke?' Lisa asked him steadily, her eyes reminding him that she was no longer a child to be placated.

For a moment she thought he was going to fob her off, but suddenly he grimaced and said, 'Bad enough—it's not a hurricane, but it isn't going to be far short. This morning's forecast suggested that we would be out of the main path. Let's just hope that things continue that way. Right now I'd feel one hell of a lot better if we could make radio contact.'

After that there wasn't much opportunity for conversation. Rorke snapped out curt orders which Lisa obeyed automatically, and between them somehow they kept the schooner on course

as the wind increased in strength and the sea ran
steadily higher, waves crashing down over the
boat's bows as she sliced swiftly through the
turbulence, but even Lisa could see that the
weather was deteriorating rather than improving.
The sky had turned a dull yellow-bronze, and
Rorke had to shout his instructions over the
keening of the wind as it tore at the sails.

'We're carrying too much sail,' he announced at
one point. 'We're running too fast. I'll have to go
and bring some in. Can you hold her on a steady
course while I do it?'

Grimly Lisa nodded. She knew without Rorke
having to put it into words that the slightest
change in wind direction could mean that they
might capsize. At the moment they were running
before the wind, but if it should veer in the
slightest and catch them sideways on, with the
amount of sail they were carrying they would
capsize immediately.

Her heart in her mouth, she struggled to keep
the schooner on course, almost jolted off her feet
when the very thing she had dreaded happened,
and the wind veered, the shock shuddering
through the slender craft with bone-jarring
ferocity. Wildly Lisa fought for control of the
helm, praying that Rorke would succeed in reefing
in some of the sail. In a few split seconds the sky
seemed to have turned almost black, the boat
wallowing and plunging in the heavy seas.

Rorke must come back soon! Lisa felt another
deep shudder tear at the schooner followed by an
ominous crack as the wind took advantage of the
boat's vulnerability to tear at the sails. She had to
go out and see what was delaying Rorke!

Setting the schooner on automatic pilot and praying that it would hold for the length of time she needed to go outside and check on Rorke, Lisa opened the door, bracing herself against the blast of the wind, feeling her way aft.

One of the sails flapped loosely, suddenly ripping free and disappearing into the darkness as she approached, and she stumbled over an obstruction on the deck. It was only as she reached out to save herself that Lisa realised the obstruction was Rorke, and that he was unconscious. Instantly she realised what had happened. The jib had obviously worked free, and when Rorke went to secure it, the wind had whipped it backwards, hitting him before he could get out of the way.

He groaned and started to struggle to his feet as Lisa reached for him, relief flooding over her as he regained consciousness.

'My God, what happened?' he muttered, getting up. 'I feel as though I've been hit by a ten-ton lorry!'

'I think it was the jib,' Lisa told him. 'The sail's gone . . .'

'Umm, I suspect you're right,' he agreed grasping her just in time to stop her staggering as the boat wallowed again.

'We'd better get below!' he shouted to her above the noise of the storm. 'We're going to have to ride this one out. We'll drop the sea anchors and take in what's left of the sails.'

Under his instructions Lisa managed to help him take in the sails, but it wasn't until they got below and he lit one of the lamps that she was able to see the damage the jib had inflicted on his skin.

His forehead was cut and grazed, blood oozing slowly from the torn flesh, and there was another matted patch of blood in his hair.

'I'll clean that up for you,' Lisa offered, trying not to let him see how concerned she was. He winced a little when she applied the antiseptic, and despite her protests insisted on going back on deck to check on the damage.

'The wind seems to have dropped a little,' he announced when he came back. 'But we won't risk putting on any more sail for now. We'll give it a little bit longer just to make sure, although I'm pretty sure we're through the worst of it.' He started to yawn, and Lisa realised how tired he must be.

'Why don't you go and rest for a while?' she suggested. 'You might as well.'

'Umm, I do feel a bit drowsy. Make sure you wake me in an hour, though, won't you?'

Lisa heard him moving about in his cabin. Soon, whenever they used the schooner, she would be sharing it with him. The thought brought her out in a rash of goosebumps. Even now she could hardly believe that he actually loved her. It all seemed like a marvellous dream.

True to Rorke's prediction, the wind dropped gradually. She looked in on him after half an hour and he was deeply asleep, his head buried against one outflung arm. A wave of melting tenderness washed over her as she looked at him, her hand reaching out to stroke the tousled hair back off his forehead. He opened his eyes and stared up at her with the unfocused blindness of the newly awake.

'Lisa?' he muttered hoarsely at last. And then his fingers were curling round her wrist, tugging her down beside him, his mouth hotly possessive as it burned against her skin, with an urgency that shattered her defences in its raw need.

'God, Lisa, I want you!' he groaned as his lips burned heatedly against the smooth skin of her throat, his hands moulding her body against the taut contours of his, tightening on her waist before sliding beneath the fine fabric of her tee-shirt to smooth the tanned skin of her midriff.

'Kiss me. Touch me,' he muttered thickly on a harshly uneven breath, and Lisa felt her body respond to the sensual demand implicit in the words, making no protest when he pushed aside the frail barrier of her tee-shirt to cup and caress the taut curves of her breasts, his thumbs stroking erotically over the already aroused nipples, until Lisa was trembling in his arms, pressing feverishly distraught kisses against his damp skin, her husky moan seeming only to incite him to further sensual forays as he removed her tee-shirt completely, his eyes darkening as he gazed down at her.

'You're so perfect I can hardly believe you're real,' he said softly at last, and then his mouth was burning a path over her skin, kindling a need within her to arch her body beneath him and entice him to possess the throbbing peaks of her breasts with the hard warmth of his hands.

His mouth stroked against her skin, the rough rasp of his beard as he explored the slender curve of her shoulder making her shiver with delicious response. Her breath caught in her throat as his lips moved questingly downwards, seeking and then finding the taut nipples he had aroused. Sensations exploded inside her as Lisa felt his

mouth against her breast. Her fingers curled
protestingly into the thick hair of his nape, her
gasp of protest checked by the spiralling pleasure
building up inside her. When she felt Rorke
tugging impatiently at the zip of her shorts, protest
couldn't have been further from her mind.

This was what she wanted; what she had been
born for, she thought wildly as she felt the feverish
urgency of his hands stroking over her stomach,
holding her, lifting her against him until she could
feel his own arousal.

His lips followed the path of his hands, shock
waves of incredulity washing over her at the
intimacy of his touch, and then he was removing his
own shorts, and the hard maleness of his body was
against hers; his skin burning with a dry heat echoed
by his lips as they moved feverishly over her skin.
Locked in his arms, Lisa could think of nothing but
that she loved him and wanted desperately to be a
part of him, even though she was surprised that he
should have chosen this moment to make her his own.

Perhaps the ferocity of the storm had reminded
him of their own mortality; and indeed, she sensed
a storm equally ferocious building up inside him as
the urgency of his lovemaking increased and she
was swept along in the fierce swell of it, unable to
reason or protest.

Rorke trembled with the pent-up force of his
desire for her, a husky groan of protest leaving his
lips before they burned against hers. His whole
body seemed to be on fire, burning against her,
turning her blood molten with need.

'Lisa, Lisa!' He muttered her name hoarsely
against her skin like a refrain, his eyes blind with
the urgency of his growing need for her. 'Lisa!'

He moaned her name against her mouth, his hands moulding her hips as he lifted her towards him and she felt the tense urgency of his need.

There was a brief searing moment of pain, lost in the sweet savagery of his possession, when they were both swept by the storm of their emotions.

Later while Rorke slept Lisa looked down at him, marvelling at their new closeness. Now they were man and wife, in deed if not in actual law, and that would soon follow. Lost in a happy daydream it was some time before she could rouse herself sufficiently to check that all was in order on deck. The storm, like their lovemaking had left behind it an oasis of perfect calm. When she went back to the cabin Rorke was still asleep sprawled on the bunk, his breathing deep and slow.

There wasn't really room for both of them on the bunk, and rather than disturb him, Lisa spent what was left of the night in her own cabin, longing for morning, longing to whisper the words of love that had trembled on her lips when he made love to her but which, then, she had been too shy to utter. How glad she was that Rorke had been her first lover. How she longed for his arms around her, his mouth on hers . . .

'Lisa . . .'

At first the deep voice was an intrusion on her dream state, and then when she opened her eyes and realised who it was who was standing there, Lisa smiled happily, taking the mug of coffee he proffered.

'Rorke . . .'

She had been about to ask him if he still loved her, but he was already turning away, his voice completely matter-of fact as he told her that the storm had died away.

He rubbed his forehead as he spoke, and Lisa noticed the bruise darkening it.

'Are you feeling okay now?' she asked him. 'I was so worried . . .'

'I'm fine. A little bit of concussion, I suspect—all I can remember is going out like a light and then nothing until I woke up this morning . . .'

'Nothing?'

Lisa stared at him. Was he teasing her?—but no, he was perfectly serious.

She took a deep breath, laughter bubbling up inside her. 'You mean you don't remember anything?'

He shrugged, heading for the door. 'No. Thanks for getting me down to my cabin, by the way—that couldn't have been easy. Nor undressing me. God knows what would have happened to me if you hadn't been there. I want to get back as fast as we can—Father will be worried.'

Now wasn't the time to discuss what had happened between them last night, and Lisa suppressed a chuckle, imagining how she would tease him later about not being able to remember their lovemaking. Concussion had strange effects on people, she knew that, and she ought perhaps to have realised the potential danger of Rorke suffering from it last night, but she had been so relieved that his injuries weren't any worse that it hadn't occurred to her.

'Breakfast in fifteen minutes,' Rorke warned her, 'and don't come on deck before—I'm going for a swim.'

What would he say if she told him that there was no need for her to stay below, that she already knew his body—intimately!

Three hours later the island was in view. There had been scant opportunity for any conversation. In fact Rorke seemed curiously tense, and once or twice Lisa had found him watching her silently.

'What's wrong?' she asked hesitantly when she saw him watching her for a third time, a curiously intent expression in his eyes. 'Have you changed your mind about—about us?'

'No, God help me,' he told her softly. 'I ought to—you're far too young to be tied down in marriage, yet, Lisa, but it's either that or make love to you anyway, and I can't see Leigh approving of that, can you?' he asked wryly.

'You want me very much?'

'More than you can imagine.' he told her succinctly. 'And desire is notorious for clouding men's minds. I ought to have sent you packing the moment I knew how I felt about you, but by then it was already too late . . .'

She took a step towards him, hoping that he would kiss her, but he had already turned away and was concentrating on bringing the schooner into the channel through the coral.

The telephone ringing woke her. She struggled downstairs to answer it, smothering a faint sigh as she recognised her agent's voice.

'Bowry's want those illustrations for the new children's series earlier than planned. How are they coming along?'

'Quite well,' she reassured him, 'but how early is "earlier"?'

'Well, I thought I'd take what you've done to show them—they went wild over that first one you did on spec.'

'Well, I'm about halfway through,' Lisa began slowly. 'Well ahead of schedule—mainly because I'd planned to give myself a week off when Robbie has his half term.' Her work was a special and private joy, partially because it enabled her to earn her own living at home, and partially because she was doing something she particularly enjoyed. When she had left home her sense of self-worth had been so low; but gradually over the months and years her self-confidence both in herself and her ability had grown. She was not under any illusions about her talent; she was never going to make the Royal Academy, but she did have enough ability to make a small name for herself and support herself and her child.

'Look, I'll come round and collect what you've done so far,' Greg suggested.

Lisa agreed, putting down the phone with a faint sigh when they had finished. Greg wouldn't be too pleased to hear what Rorke wanted her to do. She could complete her existing contract, but what would happen after that? She had a little money put by, but it wouldn't last her very long if she was forced to live on it. And yet if she refused to go; if she never saw Leigh again . . .

All morning her common sense battled with her emotions. Leigh who had stood as father to her needed her, but if she went to him she stood to lose so much; her independence not least of all.

She was still racked with indecision when Greg arrived. He gave her his usual perfunctory peck on the cheek as she let him in. Lisa smiled warmly at him. In addition to being her agent, Greg was one of her closest friends. She had met him just after Robbie's birth and although he had never said so,

Lisa knew that he believed Robbie to be the result of a brief and unhappy teenage affair. He had helped her tremendously with her work, encouraging her to persevere and eventually getting her the commissions that enabled her to work from home.

He was in his late thirties, divorced and very much a man about town. Lisa would have been blind not to notice the look in his kind brown eyes whenever they rested on her. She often wondered ironically why she was destined to attract such gentle, kind men and yet to love a far different type; a type personified by Rorke with all his inbuilt arrogance, his intense masculinity, and worst of all his wilful blindness.

'Mmm, these are very good, Lisa,' he pronounced when he had finished examining the work she had done so far. 'The best to date, I think—the expressions you've managed to put into these faces!' He indicated a group of small woodland creatures Lisa had sketched. 'I'm sure they're going to be delighted with them, Lisa, and I've got some good news—well, it could be good news. They've dropped a hint that they're looking for an artist for a new series they intend to bring out— another range of children's books, and you're a serious contender for the illustrations. They're set in Scotland—the Highlands, so you could well get a free holiday thrown in so that you can get yourself some atmosphere. I should know definitely by next week, and I'm sure these,' he waved the folio of sketches, 'will clinch it!'

'Greg——' Lisa bit her lip, pondering the best way to break the news to him, and it was only as she searched for the right words that she realised that without admitting it, subconsciously her mind was already made up—it had to be, otherwise she would not be wondering how to tell Greg that she wouldn't be going to Scotland—at least not in the immediate future.

'Lisa, is something wrong?'

She was just about to tell him when the doorbell rang.

'Want me to get it?' Greg suggested helpfully. He was standing closer to the hall door than Lisa, and she smiled her agreement rather abstractedly, still wondering how she was going to break the news to him.

The sound of Rorke's voice in the hall mingling with Greg's lighter tones shocked her. She was standing in front of the fire, her hands clasped in a gesture of subconscious supplication.

'I believe I left my gloves here last night,' Rorke announced tersely. 'I wouldn't have interrupted you, only they happened to be a gift from a close friend.'

'Helen?' Lisa queried swiftly, anger colouring her skin, her eyes glittering in an entirely feminine reaction.

'And if it was?'

Suddenly realising that Greg was watching them curiously, Lisa said levelly, 'If it was, I'm surprised you didn't take more care of them. Or were they left here simply as an excuse to come back and spy on me?'

She could tell from the dull tinge of red creeping up under his skin that her barb had found its mark.

This was the price one paid for knowing a person too well, she thought achingly. No wonder when marriages broke up it could be with such acrimony; there was nothing like intimacy to reveal the other's weaknesses and how best to make use of them.

She felt sick, hating herself for allowing her feelings to betray her into such an acid comment, but the thought of Rorke cherishing the gloves Helen had given him more than he cherished the child she had given him sickened her.

'Old friends, I take it?' Greg interrupted, watching her.

'Not friends, exactly,' Rorke replied for her, his eyes warning her to say nothing. 'Lisa is my wife.'

Lisa could tell that Greg was stunned by Rorke's statement. He looked first at Rorke and then at her for corroboration. His urgent, 'Lisa, is this true?' drew a brief nod of her head from her.

'We've been separated for years,' she said huskily, hoping he would understand all that she could not say; and forgive her for the hurt she knew she was causing him. 'I . . .'

'What I think Lisa is trying to say,' Rorke interrupted reaching for her hand and giving it a warning squeeze, 'is that we've both had a change of heart. We're going to wipe the slate clean; make a fresh start. She's coming back to the Caribbean with me.'

'Lisa?' Greg was plainly disbelieving. 'Lisa, is this true? You said nothing . . .'

'We haven't known ourselves very long,' Rorke told him coolly. 'My father is very ill, and wants to see Lisa. That was what originally brought me here.'

'Leigh has been like a father to me,' Lisa said huskily, her eyes pleading with Greg for under-standing. 'I . . .'

'Of course I understand, Lisa,' he assured her quickly. 'I suppose that means that you won't be interested in the new contract.' He sighed ruefully. 'A pity.' He turned to Rorke. 'Lisa's a very talented artist, although she tries to pretend otherwise. But then of course you'll know that.'

'I don't think Rorke is particularly interested in my artistic talents, Greg,' said Lisa in a tight voice.

'As I recall it,' Rorke drawled in a deeply suggestive tone, 'we didn't have enough time to get round to swapping hobbies.'

Even though he said nothing it struck her quite forcibly that he hadn't been surprised to hear about her work, but surely she was wrong?

'So Robbie's your son,' Greg murmured, obviously feeling ill at ease. 'There's a distinct resemblance.'

Lisa saw Rorke's mouth tighten grimly.

'Er—Lisa—look, I'd better be going. I'll take these along and see what they think.' He looked uncomfortably at Rorke. 'About the others . . .'

'I'll finish the contract, of course, Greg,' Lisa assured him, walking with him into the hall.

'I'm sorry about all this,' she apologised quietly, aware of Rorke behind her in the living room. 'It's . . .'

'Look, you don't have to explain a thing to me. I hope you'll be happy, Lisa.' Greg reached out, touching her hair and smiling wryly. 'I thought I'd give you time—not rush you because I could tell things had gone wrong for you, but it seems I took too much.'

'Touching!' Rorke sneered behind her as Lisa closed the door on Greg. The acid sound of his voice triggered off a bitter reaction, and she whirled round, anger blazing from her eyes.

How dare you sneer at Greg!' she stormed. 'Without him Robbie and I could never have managed!'

'Typical of you,' Rorke grimaced. 'That's your standby isn't it, Lisa, find another man to shoulder your responsibilities.'

'Don't you mean *your* responsibilities, Rorke?' Lisa flung at him. 'Yes, that's right' she told him bitterly. 'Robbie is your child—your child, Rorke, and nothing you can say or do can alter that, no matter how much you may want it to.'

'Still sticking to the same old story? Come on, Lisa, we both know I'm not Robbie's father, don't we?'

'Mummy, Mummy, I'm home!'

Lisa bit back the angry words she had been about to utter and turned to welcome Robbie with a hug and a kiss.

She had a neighbour with whom she shared the chore of taking Robbie and his friend Jonathan to and from school, and Robbie was full of the day's happenings, pausing briefly to glance uncertainly at Rorke before continuing with his saga.

Lisa listened, but all the time her heart was thudding as though she had been running. Robbie was Rorke's son; dear God, she had thought she was over the agony of hearing him deny it, but it was still as fresh as ever; the anguish of Rorke's rejection of them both still just as intense. She could remember every detail of those days leading up to her flight from the Caribbean.

CHAPTER FOUR

AT the time it had all seemed to happen so quickly—as quickly and without warning as the storms that swept the Caribbean, but with hindsight and maturity Lisa had come to accept that the love she had thought so shining and perfect had been flawed almost from the very start. For one thing there had been Rorke's resentment of her; she had been too blind to see it at the time, but when she looked back . . .

Even now it made her throat ache to remember how happy she had been when they returned to the island. Leigh had been there to greet them, and she had blurted out their news, seeing her joy reflected in his eyes. Had it been Leigh who had suggested the engagement party? She seemed to remember that Rorke had demurred, but it had never crossed her mind, then, that he might be having second thoughts. It had taken Helen to point that out to her; to feed the poison of doubt to her drop by drop.

She hadn't even been unduly concerned that Rorke couldn't remember their lovemaking. She had quizzed Mike discreetly about concussion and its after-effects, and had been satisfied enough, then, with his description of its effects not to worry too much about Rorke's loss of memory. It would come back to him, she felt sure, and then they would laugh together about it. Had his memory of what happened between them ever resurfaced? Lisa wondered bitterly, watching him as Robbie trotted over to him, completely unawed and quite obviously a little bit excited about the advent of this strange male into his young life. If it had would Rorke deliberately repress it; refuse to admit how he had wronged her, and more important than her, wronged Robbie? Rorke's family had owned St Martins for many generations; it was Robbie's birthright that Rorke had deprived him of when he deprived him of his name, but it wasn't Robbie's loss of possessions that upset Lisa, it was the fact that he would never know the love of his father. Of course the little boy had been curious and she had striven to answer his questions as honestly as she could. He knew he had a daddy who lived a long way away, and mercifully beyond that he had not questioned her. Lisa was no fool, though. The day would come when he would want to know more, and now here was Rorke, bringing that day closer by insisting that they return with him to the island.

Could she go back? Had she strength to return to the place where she had known such delirious happiness, and such bitter pain?

'Come back, Lisa, you were miles away,' Rorke's voice goaded. 'Where, I wonder? In the arms of your lover?'

Lisa's mouth compressed in a tight line,

'I've only had one lover, Rorke,' she told him levelly.

'You mean you expect me to believe there's been no one else since Peters?' he mocked, deliberately misunderstanding. 'Why? After all, you were willing enough to go to bed with me, before I found out the truth.'

'The truth?' Lisa stormed, the cold condemnation in his eyes and voice suddenly unleashing a torrent of rage—against Rorke himself, against his wilful blindness, against Helen who had destroyed their marriage almost before it got started, but most of all against Rorke, for his lack of faith, of trust, and surely love, because if he had truly loved her he would have believed her.

'Mummy!' Robbie wailed, sensing the antagonism springing up between the two adults. 'Mummy!'

'Don't cry, Robbie, everything's all right.'

'He loves you now, Lisa,' Rorke said softly, as she bent to pick Robbie up, 'but will he still love you when he learns the truth about his daddy?'

'I know about my daddy,' Robbie piped up shrilly, fixing his eyes on Rorke. 'He lives a long way away, over the sea. That's why we never see him. Jamie has a new daddy,' he announced gravely to Lisa. 'Will I ever have a new daddy?'

Out of the corner of her eye Lisa saw Rorke's mouth tighten.

'It's time for Robbie's lunch,' she told him. 'We can't talk now, Rorke. I've got some work to do this afternoon.'

'Then I'll come back this evening, and when I do, I expect to get an answer from you, Lisa. Don't forget, will you, that if Robbie were my child, I'd be able to take him back with me, with or without your permission, and if that's what it takes to get you to see Dad, then that's exactly what I'll do. He needs you, Lisa.'

Long after Rorke was gone and Robbie was back at school, Lisa still heard those words. Leigh needed her. Could she refuse to go to him? Did she really want to? When Rorke had refused to accept that she was expecting his child she had run away, unable to stay, and, she acknowledged, in some ways she had been running ever since. Perhaps now the time had come to stop. She pushed away her work, unable to concentrate. Tonight Rorke would be back, wanting her answer.

She sighed, and got up, not seeing the neat living room, but instead the high-ceilinged gracious rooms of Rorke's home on St Martins.

It was there that their engagement had been announced. Rorke had been withdrawn even then. She had overheard him complaining to his father that he hadn't wanted all this fuss, just a quiet, simple wedding. Lisa hadn't heard Leigh's response; she hadn't wanted to eavesdrop, but her heart had been warmed by Rorke's admission, coming after several days when he had done nothing more than give her his customary brotherly kiss at breakfast and again at night, making no attempt to be alone with her.

She had intended to go to him and tell him that she too wanted them to be married quietly, but before she was able to do so he had been called away to one of their hotels.

It had been while he was away that she discovered she was pregnant. She had been feeling nauseous in the morning for several days, but had thought nothing of it until one afternoon when she had gone up to the hospital to help out by chatting to the patients and generally making herself useful. It had been unusually hot, but that alone did not account for the sudden faintness that overcame her; it had taken Mike to point out the truth to her, gently and with considerable concern. He had wanted her to be completely sure, and Lisa had agreed to go with him to his bungalow where he had a small surgery and where there would be less chance of anyone else guessing.

The examination had been over in minutes. Mike had been entirely professional, and Lisa trusted him completely, but there had been a hard edge of anger to his voice when he asked abruptly when he had finished, 'What the hell was Rorke thinking about? A man of his experience, surely he . . .'

'Rorke doesn't know,' Lisa was quick to correct him, to defend her beloved Rorke from his disapproval, the words tumbling out of her mouth as she explained blushingly what had happened.

A little to her surprise Mike looked very grave.

'Concussion is a very strange thing, Lisa,' he said slowly when she had finished. 'You must realise there's no guarantee that Rorke will ever remember.'

'But he'll know anyway when I tell him,' Lisa pointed out, to her mind logically. 'And then there's the baby . . .'

'Yes.'

Mike seemed very abstracted, and the first frisson of fear had shivered over her.

'Lisa, I don't pretend to be any kind of psychiatrist, but it strikes me as odd that Rorke should choose to blot out such a very personal memory. I . . .'

'Choose?' Lisa had demanded, instantly picking him up. 'But you just said that concussion . . .'

'Yes, I know what I said,' Mike agree, 'but I think there's more to it than that. I think you must tell Rorke straight away about what happened, and about the baby. Lisa, try to understand. Rorke's been away one hell of a lot just recently, hasn't he?' He had given her a direct look. 'Rorke's a man in his late twenties, Lisa, and you're a girl of seventeen. He loves you, he's going to marry you, and so it follows like night follows day that he wants you—and probably very badly. What I'm trying to tell you is that he's probably been keeping away from you deliberately, restraining himself because ... Oh, hell!' he broke off angrily.

'But there's no need for him to keep me at a distance, we've already made love,' Lisa had pointed out, frowning.

'Exactly,' Mike had agreed. 'And what do you think it's going to do to him to discover that he's already violated the innocence he's trying so damned hard to protect. No wonder he can't remember—He's a very complex character Lisa, and at a guess I'd say he probably feels very conscious of the age gap between you. You're still a child; he's been an elder-brother, protector figure to you for so long that you can't blame him if he finds it difficult to make the adjustment from brother to lover, however much he wants you.'

'You mean he won't believe me?' Lisa had whispered, her throat dry with tension and fear.

'Oh, I'm not saying that,' Mike had been quick to comfort her. 'Of course he'll believe you, but my guess is that he won't like himself much—at least for a while. He's a tough character, Lisa, with a will as strong as steel, and something tells me he's going to find it hard to forgive himself this.'

He had seen the tears forming in her eyes and

had leaned forward to comfort her, holding her gently against his shoulder, and that had been when Rorke had walked in. Lisa had seen him first, over Mike's shoulder, stubble darkening his jaw, his eyes smouldering with an emotion she couldn't define.

She had left with him, tense and on edge, dreading having to tell him about the baby, wondering how on earth she was to find the right words.

To make matters worse Helen had been at the house when they got back. She had travelled over from St Lucia with Rorke, and Lisa had felt red-hot jealousy claw at her when Helen mentioned that they had spent a couple of days together on St Lucia. She was doing it deliberately to make her jealous, Lisa told herself stoutly. She knew that Rorke had been working. She only had to look at Rorke's tired features to know that. But that didn't stop the pain, nor the ache of doubt that still lingered from her talk with Mike.

Later that night she had heard someone outside her door. Thinking it might be Rorke, she had sat up excitedly, her face eager, but it had been Helen who stepped through the door, Helen, her face alight with triumph, her voice a low purr as she said venomously, 'Expecting Rorke? My dear, if you had that sort of relationship with him he would hardly be marrying you, would he? Rorke is a realist first and last. He's marrying you because he wants you and he can't get you any other way. Also you're the sort of wife his father approves of, but don't deceive yourself that he loves you, Lisa. Rorke loves me, and he'll come back to me when he's grown tired of making love to a child. Your innocence might be a challenge now, but . . .'

Unable to bear the other woman's mockery, Lisa had burst out, 'What makes you think that Rorke and I aren't already lovers?'

Helen's smile had been openly derisive. 'If you are, it can't have been very successful, otherwise why would Rorke have come to St Lucia—to me, Lisa?'

She could still remember the pain of it now, the desire to scream that Helen was lying, but she hadn't been able to, and instead it had been Helen who had the last word, saying spitefully, 'A final word of warning, my dear—Rorke doesn't like sharing, and if you're wise you'll keep your . . . friendship . . . with our handsome young doctor a secret from him.'

Helen had stayed for two days, monopolising Rorke, excluding Lisa from everything they did together. Plans for the wedding went ahead, and Lisa was aware of Leigh watching her with concern in his eyes as she had tried to hide her despair and misery from everyone, longing only for the opportunity to talk to Rorke, to tell him about the night on board *Lady* and the repercussions from it, but he was strangely elusive. It was almost as though he didn't want to talk to her.

The night Helen left Lisa waited until the others had gone to bed and then followed Rorke to his room. She had knocked and then entered without waiting for him to call out. He had been standing in the middle of the room when she opened the door, his shirt already off, moonlight silvering the streamlined muscles of his torso. Her body had clenched in unwilling excitement, her mouth unbearably dry as she looked at him.

His heavy-lidded glance swept over her, and in

sudden heated urgency Lisa murmured his name, closing her eyes as she swayed towards him, feeling the hard band of his arms tightening round her as he swore under his breath, and then her cheek was against the cool skin of his shoulder, and she was breathing in the warm male scent of his body.

'Lisa, what is it?' she heard him demand above her, and her whole body started to tremble, her pulses leaping in response to the raw thread of sensuality running through his words.

'Lisa, can't you feel what you're doing to me?' Rorke muttered thickly against her hair.

'I want to talk to you.' There, the words were out, but Rorke ignored them, laughing savagely, as he released her and snapped on the light.

'Not tonight you don't, Lisa. Go to bed,' he told her, his voice suddenly harsh, 'before I forget all the promises I've made myself and take you to mine. Go, Lisa,' he had told her harshly, and because of what she had read in his face she had fled, tears streaming down her face as she curled up in her own cold bed, wondering if Helen had been right and Rorke was simply marrying her because he wanted her physically.

Too bemused and confused to rationalise her thoughts, she had at last fallen asleep, wishing childishly that somehow during the night all would be made well and when she woke up all the dark clouds would have vanished.

It was just after eight when Rorke returned. Lisa had just finished putting Robbie to bed.

She refused to look at him as she let him in, but somehow his tall frame drew her eyes as he followed her into the small living room. He had changed into narrow dark cords and a checked woollen shirt which stretched tightly across his shoulders. He was carrying a leather blouson which he tossed casually on to a chair before sitting down.

'Do make yourself at home,' Lisa gritted sarcastically.

'Thanks, I will.'

He seemed impervious to her anger—but then he had always been impervious, she just hadn't recognised the fact.

'I can't stay long,' he told her coolly, flicking back his cuff to study his watch, 'I've got an appointment later.'

'Who with, Helen? Is she with you?'

'Hardly. After all, in the eyes of the world I'm still a married man.'

'Just as you were an engaged man when you spent two days with Helen on St Lucia,' Lisa told him huskily, 'and you needn't bother denying it— Helen told me herself, just as she told me why you wanted to marry me. But she was right, wasn't she, Rorke? You didn't love me. All you wanted to do was to possess me.'

'Always supposing you're right, I didn't get what you said I wanted, did I? Although you were willing enough to give yourself to someone else, as I recall. I even found the two of you together in his bungalow. Helen was right to warn me. Perhaps she was also right to tell me I should simply have taken you, the way he did.'

'Mike never touched me!' Lisa objected furiously.

So it had been Helen who had hinted to Rorke

that she and Mike were lovers. She had always suspected it.

'No? But someone did, didn't they? I asked you on our wedding night if you were coming to me a virgin, and you told me "no".'

'Because you and I had already been lovers,' Lisa told him, her voice huskily taut with the need to make him see the truth.

'Oh, for God's sake!' A cynical grimace curved his mouth downwards. 'Don't give me all that again! How I made love to you on board *Lady*, and then couldn't remember a damn thing about it. Not remember!' He laughed mirthlessly. 'God, if you knew how much I wanted you, you'd never say that! You were almost an obsession with me, Lisa. I tried telling myself you were just a child—my sister almost, but none of it did any good, I just had to look at you and I burned; burned up with wanting you, and you're trying to tell me I wouldn't remember touching you, fathering your child. Have you any idea what I put myself through in those days before the wedding, trying to protect you from myself? Nights without sleep, aching for the day, days working myself into the ground so that I could blot you out of my mind. Even promising my father that I wouldn't rush you, wouldn't frighten you with my need for you. And then I find out that it was all a sham; that the innocence I'd been killing myself to protect simply didn't exist. And you try to convince me that I was the one? God, Lisa,' he muttered, his face suddenly dark and congested with a bitter fury, 'do you think I wouldn't know if I'd made love to you? Do you think my body wouldn't tell me? Do you think I'd ever forgive myself if I thought there was the slightest chance that you're telling the truth?'

Lisa had been about to retaliate when the meaning of Rorke's final words penetrated. She knew he was telling the truth; she could hear the anguish in his voice, see it in his eyes.

'Don't you think I tried to believe it?' Rorke demanded roughly. 'God knows I wanted to, but I swore to myself before we left St Lucia that I wouldn't touch you. I made myself a promise that I'd wait until we were married, until I could woo you properly, without frightening or alarming you, and then you turn round and tell me that I possessed you on *Lady*. How the hell do you think I could live with myself if I thought for one single moment that that was true?'

There was nothing she could say. She knew he spoke the truth; it probably would destroy him if he found out that he had been wrong, and suddenly the image she had held in her mind all those years since Robbie's birth, of Rorke coming to her, admitting that he had been wrong, telling her he wanted them both back, that he couldn't live without them, melted, and Lisa knew agonisingly that his knowing the truth would simply make a wider gulf between them.

Rorke genuinely believed that he could not, would not have made love to her, and she could see with a mature wisdom she had lacked at the time that to discover the truth now would destroy his own faith in himself. And anyway, what did it matter? she asked herself wearily. He didn't love her; had probably never loved her as she had him. He had wanted her. He was quite frank about that; and she, in her youthful innocence, had assumed that 'wanting' and 'loving' were synonymous. Now she knew better, and she could also see what Mike had been getting at when he had tried to warn her how difficult it might be to get Rorke to accept the truth.

'Well, Lisa?' she heard Rorke demanding roughly. 'Are you going to come back with me?'

'Won't Helen have something to say about that?'

'My relationship with Helen is strictly out of bounds as far as you're concerned. For all that you may deride her, Lisa, at least she's honest in what she is.'

'Oh yes,' she flung back at him, suddenly infuriated by his defence of the other woman. 'And it's all right for Helen to sleep with whoever she wants—you can't tell me you're the only lover she's ever had, but simply because you think I ...'

'It wasn't your virginity, damn you!' Rorke gritted, a dark tide of colour creeping up under his skin, as he reached for her, fingers circling her wrists like a steel clamp.

'No?' Lisa said shakily, trying to twist free. 'You'll have to forgive me if I think differently, Rorke—after all, the facts speak for themselves. You were pretty quick to point out that you didn't want "another man's leavings"—that was the polite way you described me, as I remember.'

'You were my wife!' Rorke was breathing heavily, his eyes dark with remembered rage. 'I'd torn myself apart trying to protect you, trying ... Oh, for God's sake what's the use? What really galled me was not so much what you'd done, but the way you tried to deceive me, to tear me apart by telling me it was me, and then trying to foist Peters' brat off on me.'

The sharp sound of Lisa's open palm connecting

with his jaw echoed through the small room, her face as white as milk as she stared blindly up at him.

She was trembling in fear and shock. She had never employed physical violence in all her life, and yet for one brief second of time she had found pleasure and release in the sting of her palm against Rorke's face.

'Why, you . . .!'

She was yanked bodily into Rorke's arms, her heart pounding in terror as they locked round her and she was forced backwards against his arm, his hand lifting to grasp her chin and lift her face so that he could look into her eyes.

'What's the matter?' he asked insultingly, studying her hectically flushed cheeks and glittering eyes. 'Isn't Greg a satisfactory lover, or is it simply that you like a little bit of variety, because that's what all that was about, wasn't it, Lisa? You wanted to be here in my arms, didn't you?'

'No!' she denied vehemently. How could he think such a thing? Her whole body was trembling helplessly and fear crawled down her spine as he looked at her. 'I wouldn't want you to touch me if . . . if you were the last man on earth!' she snapped childishly. 'Helen might go in for those sort of games, but I don't. Now perhaps you'll let me go.' She tilted her chin proudly, defying him to refuse.

'Helen's all woman,' he drawled, ignoring her demand. 'She doesn't have to play games to get across what she wants. It's been five years, Lisa, and I reckon you owe me this.'

He bent his head and she could see the dark flecks in his eyes, the hard purpose of his mouth as it closed on hers, ruthlessly determined to shatter

her defences and impose its superior male strength.
It wasn't a kiss of desire, Lisa recognised as she
fought its dominance, it was a punishment, a
brand, a pain that burned itself into her heart and
left her crying silently inside, her lips bruised and
swollen when Rorke released them.

'I have to go now,' he told her emotionlessly.
'But I'll be back, and when I come back I want
your answer.'

'And if it's "no"?' Lisa demanded huskily.

For a moment she thought he actually intended
to strike her, and took an instinctive step
backwards. Rorke's mouth curled sardonically as
he recognised her fear.

'Like I said, a man's entitled to the company of
his only child—if you've any sense you'll come,
Lisa. You obviously love your son, even if you
don't give a damn for my father.'

He was gone before she could retort, leaving her
bruised in body and spirit, wishing he had never
come back into her life, wondering why on earth
she had not punished him with the truth—because
it would be a punishment to him to discover it.
What a fool she was to allow the residue of old
emotions to trap her into a desire to protect rather
than to hurt. Hurt! Didn't Rorke deserve to be
hurt after what he had done to her? And yet she
knew she could never be the one to retaliate. She
just didn't have it in her.

CHAPTER FIVE

'Mummy, Mummy, wake up!'

Drowsily, Lisa surfaced from sleep. Robbie was standing beside her bed, his small face determined, the blue-green eyes, all that he had inherited from her, looking accusingly at her.

'Why are you still sleeping?' he demanded, watching her. 'I've been awake for ages!'

He had tried to dress himself, and a strong surge of love tugged at her body as Lisa propped herself up on one elbow to watch him. He was so sturdy and self-assured, this son of hers; so much his father's child in everything he did. But Rorke would never acknowledge him. To Rorke he was Mike's child. The thick dark hair, so like his father's, tangled and unruly, curled round his still babyish little boy's face, but despite the baby chubbiness, already in his bone structure Lisa could recognise Rorke's.

A rattle in the hall heralded the arrival of the post, and suppressing a sigh Lisa swung her legs out of bed, as Robbie hurried downstairs to see what had arrived.

Lisa heard him coming back as she stepped into the shower. He was talking to himself; she could hear the high piping voice, and she smiled to herself, picturing him climbing the stairs. He still had to take them one at a time, and consequently it took him a couple of minutes to reach the top. She heard him pushing open the bathroom door, and called out to him to pass her a towel as she turned off the shower and opened the door. Her body stiffened as she realised that Robbie wasn't alone. Rorke was with him, and it was Rorke who proffered the towel she had asked for, galvanising her tense muscles into action as she whipped the towel round her, securing it like a sarong, as she darted Rorke a look of bitter hatred.

'What are you doing here?' she hissed as she urged Robbie towards the door. 'How did you get in?'

'Robbie let me in,' Rorke told her calmly, apparently completely undisturbed by the intimacy of their surroundings.

'I want my breakfast,' Robbie announced, looking from one adult face to the other.

'Go down stairs, Robbie, I'll be down in a minute,' Lisa instructed, glancing coldly and pointedly at Rorke as he followed her on to the landing.

'If you don't mind,' she told him icily, 'I'd like to get dressed. 'I realise that good manners are apparently completely alien to you—otherwise you'd never have come up here in the first place,' she added when he refused to move, 'but getting dressed is something I prefer to do without an audience.'

'You surprise me,' was Rorke's cynical comment, as he stepped past her, and as she opened her bedroom door Lisa found she was shaking with a mixture of temper and reaction. Just for a moment as she stepped out of the shower and saw Rorke there time had telescoped, present and past mingling, and just briefly, for the merest heartbeat, she had experienced again all those emotions she had known at seventeen.

But she wasn't seventeen any longer. She was twenty-two and the mother of a five-year-old son whose father refused to acknowledge him, and that was somthing she would be wise not to forget.

She dressed quickly in jeans and a checked shirt. The jeans were relatively new ones and emphasised the slender length of her legs. Her hair, tangled and slightly damp from the shower, curled riotously on to her shoulders, and with an impatient gesture she tied it back into one long plait, securing it with a rubber band.

As she reached the kitchen she could smell coffee and toast. She pushed open the door, and the domesticity of the scene that greeted her took her by the throat, reminding her of how very vulnerable she still was no matter how much she might want to deny it. Robbie was sitting in his chair, eating toast. Rorke was standing beside him talking to him. Both of them looked up as she walked in, identical expressions in their eyes. If Rorke could see what she could see he would never imagine that Robbie was anyone else's child. But he didn't want to know about Robbie's parenthood, she reminded herself, hardening her heart. He had wanted to believe what Helen had told him. Perhaps he had even then been regretting marrying her; wanting a way out. He had certainly never made any attempt to find her before—and now that he had it was for Leigh's sake, not his own.

'We're going to fly a long way in a huge plane,' Robbie told her matter-of-factly as she sat down, adding innocently, 'We're going with my daddy.'

Lisa's head shot up, her eyes widening in shock.

'It's all right,' Rorke announced, anticipating her. 'I've explained to Robbie that I'm his father.'

'You never told me much about my daddy,' Robbie interrupted, accusingly. 'You said it was mostly the two of us, Mummy.'

Oh, for the logic of youth, Lisa thought on a sigh, choking down the fierce wave of anger she felt against Rorke. How dared he walk calmly into her life, throwing out orders, telling Robbie that he was his father, carelessly and casually, not giving a thought to the effect it was likely to have on the little boy once he discovered the true situation?

'Something wrong?' Rorke had followed her across to the sink, watching her fill the kettle with hands that trembled betrayingly.

'Of course there is,' Lisa whispered savagely. 'How dare you tell Robbie that you're his father!'

'If he doesn't believe it, no one else is going to,' Rorke told her quietly, 'and I won't have my father upset, Lisa. It's imperative that he's given some reason to hold on to life, that's what the experts say, and I'm hoping that Robbie will prove to be that reason.'

'You planned this, didn't you?' Lisa said bitterly. 'You didn't come here to take me back at all. You wanted Robbie . . .'

'My father wants you both,' Rorke corrected. A muscle beat angrily in his jaw and Lisa wondered at his hardness, his ability to ride roughshod over everyone else simply to get what he wanted.

'So you knew about Robbie?' she ventured bitterly.

'I knew you were carrying a child—you told me so yourself, remember?'

She darted a look at the hard, implacably set features and wondered at his control over his emotions. He hated her, she knew that, and yet for his father's sake he was prepared to take her back to St Martins and Robbie with him, acknowledging Robbie as his son, even though he believed him to be Mike's.

But Robbie was his son, and had every right to live on St Martins; every right to expect to be treated as Rorke's son, and she did not have the ability to deprive her child of that right, Lisa decided achingly.

'It's perfectly all right, Lisa,' Rorke said softly, watching the play of emotions over her face. 'I've never believed in punishing the child for the crimes of its parents, and Robbie won't suffer for his fathering at my hands. Besides, all I'm concerned with here is my father and his return to health.'

'And to ensure that you're prepared to suffer my presence on St Martins, is that it?' Lisa demanded in a choked voice. God, his arrogance made her long to hit him!

'You're the one who said it,' Rorke drawled insultingly. 'But yes. For my father's sake, I'm prepared to do what I said I never would do, and that is to accept your son as my child.'

'Big of you,' Lisa muttered under her breath. 'I'm sure Robbie will be most appreciative, if you're around long enough for him to realise the sacrifice that you've made. Couldn't you simply have told him that you were a friend? Children aren't fools. Robbie is already aware of the fact that there's only me—like all children he's inquisitive and curious. Now you've told him you're his father, he will expect you to *be* his father.'

Was he remembering as she was that he had
sworn he would never acknowledge Robbie as his
son?

'And so I will be—at least for as long as you're
on St Martins.'

But what about after that? Lisa wondered with
an aching heart. She was under no illusions. Rorke
was simply using them to protect his father, and
once Leigh recovered they would be cruelly and
firmly jettisoned. For herself, she could cope—no
pain could ever equal what she had experienced
when she first left Rorke, but it was Robbie she
was worried about now. Robbie who would suffer
dreadfully if he was allowed to get too close to
Rorke; if he did indeed come to accept Rorke as
his father, and Lisa made a private vow that no
matter what Rorke might tell the little boy she
would do all she could to protect him.

'I've booked us on the evening flight,' Rorke
told her. 'You'll need to do some shopping—buy
Robbie some lightweight clothes, etc. I've telephoned home to tell them to expect us. If you
manage to persuade my father to have this
operation I'm willing to be very generous to you,
Lisa.' He looked round the small, cramped room,
his glance indicating how easily he thought she
would be tempted by his suggestion.

Anger, molten hot and bitter, churned through
her.

'Whatever I do, I'm doing for Leigh, not for
you, Rorke,' she threw at him, 'and I don't need
bribing. I love Leigh . . .'

'So much that you ran out on me and never
even let him know where you were. Some love!'
Rorke sneered. 'Didn't you ever think about what

you were doing to him? About the gossip that would ensue, especially when Mike Peters left the island only weeks after you?'

Mike had left the island? That was something she hadn't known.

'Don't come the innocent with me,' Rorke snarled. 'I know the two of you were together in Paris. Helen saw you when she was on a buying trip. She let it slip . . .'

'I can imagine,' Lisa retorted hotly. 'But she happens to have been lying. I haven't seen Mike since I left St Martin's.'

Rorke shrugged, plainly losing interest in the subject, and Lisa suddenly became aware of Robbie, who was watching with rounded eyes.

'Why are you getting cross, Mummy?' he demanded suspiciously. 'Are you cross with my daddy?'

His lower lip trembled a little, and Lisa bit her lip, mentally chiding herself for letting Robbie witness their quarrel.

She was just about to reassure the little boy, when to her surprise Rorke scooped him up into his arms, holding him level with his face.

'Mummy and I were just talking,' he lied reassuringly. 'It just sounded as though Mummy was getting cross.'

The explanation seemed to satisfy Robbie, and Lisa, who sometimes found his inescapable thirst for knowledge wearying, suppressed a small spurt of resentment that he should accept Rorke and his explanation so readily.

Robbie, though, was apparently engrossed in other matters. 'If you're my daddy, why haven't you been to see me before?' he asked queryingly.

'I haven't been able to,' Rorke told him easily, 'but I'm here now, and . . .'

'And you're going to take us home with you,' Robbie supplied, obviously having been well primed. 'My daddy lives on a real island,' he told Lisa importantly,' and I'll be able to learn to swim properly. Will I have to go to school?'

School! That was something Lisa hadn't thought about, but she suspected they wouldn't be there long enough for her to need to worry too much about the time Robbie might miss off school. However, to her surprise, Rorke responded immediately, 'There's a school on the island, Robbie—you'll like it, I know, and then when you're older you'll go to school here in England like I did.'

He saw Lisa glaring at him, and put Robbie back on the floor. The little boy quickly became engrossed in his toys, leaving Lisa free to whisper bitterly, 'Did you have to tell him that? He has an excellent memory, Rorke, and you said you didn't want to punish him for my sins. How do you think he's going to feel when he realises you've lied to him? That you're just using us?'

'We'll cross that bridge when we come to it,' Rorke told her, adding cynically, 'What upsets you the most, Lisa? The fact that I might be hurting Robbie, or the fact that he could so easily have been my child if only Helen hadn't told me the truth.'

'The truth?' Lisa laughed bitterly. 'What do you know about the truth, Rorke? Nothing! Nothing at all!'

If she had any sense, she would refuse here and now to go back to St Martins with him, but the thought of Leigh tugged at her heartstrings. Leigh and Robbie, who would surely find much pleasure in one another. Could she, merely for selfish reasons of her own, deny them that relationship? In her heart of hearts she already knew the answer.

It was a hectic rush to be ready on time, and in the end, much to her surprise, Rorke suggested that he looked after Robbie while she did her shopping.

It wasn't easy finding lightweight clothes for a small boy in mid-November, but at last it was all done, and after all, they wouldn't be on St Martin's for very long, Lisa assured herself as she hurried homewards.

It was growing dark as she walked along the road, and as she opened her gate she absently noted the familiar squeak. She would have to go next door and ask her neighbour to keep an eye on the house while she was away.

She pushed open the living room door, unprepared for the scene that met her eyes. Rorke was relaxing in one of the armchairs, Robbie asleep on his lap, and something about the totally relaxed and trusting face of her son made Lisa's heart ache for all that she had lost. Quickly she dismissed the thought. It was not her fault if Rorke had refused to believe her; if he chose to believe Helen instead.

Something about the sleeping man drew her. She bent forward almost instinctively, her heart thudding as Rorke's eyes opened. Just for a second they looked at one another, and then Rorke said dangerously softly, 'Wondering how you're going to manage without Greg? He is your latest lover, I presume.' He said it so sardonically that Lisa felt anger flare hotly inside her, provoking her to retort bitterly,

'Why the hell should I tell you? At least he's honest and decent, which is more than I can say for Helen! I assume she is still the woman in your life?' she added recklessly.

'And if she is? You wouldn't by any chance be jealous, would you, Lisa?'

'Of what? Helen enjoying your prowess as a lover? As according to you I've never known that pleasure, I've nothing to be jealous of, have I?'

She had caught him off guard, Lisa thought with satisfaction, but in another moment he had himself under control, his expression mocking as he drawled softly, 'Hasn't anyone ever told you what a powerful aphrodisiac the imagination can be, Lisa?'

His mockery infuriated her and she flung at him bitterly, 'If you think I've ever imagined you making love to me . . .'

'Haven't you?' he interrupted softly, watching her flushed cheeks and glittering eyes. 'Haven't you, Lisa?'

Her expression gave her away, she knew. She licked her lips nervously, suddenly unbearably reminded of all those occasions when she had lain sleepless, reliving the touch of Rorke's hands on her body, the hungry possession of his mouth. Perspiration broke out on her skin, her eyes drawn to the hard line of his mouth. Her body started to tremble, and a curious weakness robbed her of the ability to think logically. Rorke was watching her narrowly, his eyes on the parted warmth of her mouth. She swayed towards him, then suddenly

Robbie stirred in her arms, breaking the spell which had held her in thrall. Rorke stepped back, his eyes cruelly cynical.

'Careful, Lisa,' he warned her bitingly. 'You're a woman now, with all a woman's desires, but I'm not going to appease them for you.'

She was still trying to think of a fitting retort when he opened the door and walked out.

'Mummy, I'm tired! When will we be there?'

'Not long now, Robbie,' Rorke soothed him, lifting his head from the papers he had been studying ever since they boarded the aircraft. It was a long flight for so young a child, and now Robbie was starting to grow restless.

'We'll spend tonight on St Lucia,' Rorke announced. '*Lady* is berthed at Castries, and we'll sail from there in the morning.'

'*Lady?*' Lisa mumbled. 'You've still got her?'

'What the hell did you expect me to do with her?' Rorke retorted, looking cynically amused. 'Scuttle her like a heartbroken idiot? She's too valuable for that. I charter her a good deal these days.' His mouth twisted. 'She's very popular for honeymoon cruises.'

'What's a honeymoon, Mummy?' Robbie demanded, pouncing on the new word with interest.

'It's a sort of holiday,' Lisa replied vaguely, glad when something else caught his attention. How long did Rorke intend to keep them on St Martin's? How long would it be before Leigh was well enough for them to leave? These were questions she should have asked in London, but somehow there hadn't been time.

'Tell me about Leigh,' she turned to Rorke. 'How serious is it?'

'Serious enough to warrant him being hospitalised in intensive care on Martinique,' Rorke told her grimly. 'They wanted him to have an operation then, but he refused. He wanted to see you,' he told her bleakly, 'and he knew there was only a fifty per cent chance of survival.'

Tears stung her eyes. Dear Leigh! How she had missed him. Only now would she let herself admit how much.

'Does he know about Robbie?' She asked the question without looking at Rorke.

'Not from me, so he's going to be a welcome bonus. I'll tell him that you only discovered you were pregnant after our quarrel—which is quite conceivable, since, as far as he's aware, you ran away from me after one night of wedded bliss. I shall tell him that you didn't tell me about Robbie, and then when I came to find you to tell you about his accident, the joy of discovering my wife and child was so great that I simply had to persuade you to agree to a reconciliation.'

'You think he'll believe that?'

Rorke smiled cynically. 'He wants to believe it, Lisa, and he'll want to believe it even more when he finds out about Robbie.'

'And you're prepared to let him believe that Robbie is your son, after all that you said?'

'He's my father, and I want him to live. I seem to think that letting him know that the sweet, innocent child he cherished as a daughter was neither of those things, and that, moreover, she is the mother of an illegitimate child is hardly likely to achieve that aim, do you?'

'And what about Helen?' Lisa asked in a low voice. 'Are you going to tell her the truth?'

'Your presence on St Martins is hardly likely to affect Helen,' Rorke told her cruelly, 'and neither is my relationship with her any business of yours.'

Two hours later they were touching down on St Lucia. The heat was something Lisa had almost forgotten. It hit them in a burning, dry wave as they stepped off the plane and waited to go through Customs.

Mercifully, Rorke was recognised and they were waved through after the merest formalities. Robbie rubbed tiredly at his eyes as Rorke led the way to a waiting Range Rover, lifting the little boy inside and making sure he was comfortable before turning back to Lisa. He was just on the point of helping her into the Range Rover when a bright scarlet sports car pulled up beside them with a spurt of gravel sending up miniature clouds of dust. Lisa felt her stomach muscles tense as she recognised Helen's titian hair, and then the other woman was out of the car, hurrying welcomingly towards Rorke, ignoring Lisa as she lifted her face for his kiss. Time seemed to roll back; she was sixteen again, gauche and nervous, only this time she had the added handicap of jet flight exhaustion, and the sensation of grubbiness and loss of energy peculiar to long flights to contend with.

'Rorke, I'm so pleased I've caught you,' Helen said huskily. 'I've come straight from Castries. There's been been a problem with *Lady*. Something to do with one of the engines, but they're working on it now. You don't have her chartered for a couple of weeks, do you?'

Did Helen have to stress so obviously how intimately she was involved in Rorke's day-to-day life? Lisa wondered acidly. Robbie was watching them from the Range Rover, and she moved across to reassure him that he hadn't been deserted. Helen was watching her and Lisa had the satisfaction of seeing the other woman's face pale with shock as she recognised Rorke's distinctive features on his son in miniature.

'Lisa,' she acknowledged briefly. 'Quite a surprise to see you back.'

'Yes, I'm sure it must be,' Lisa agreed equally sweetly. 'Robbie, say hello to Helen.'

'Hello,' Robbie obliged, round-eyed. 'Are you one of Daddy's friends?'

Helen blanched and for a moment Lisa almost felt sorry as she saw the other woman turn accusingly to Rorke.

'He called you "Daddy"!' she snapped angrily to Rorke. 'What's going on? You said nothing about bringing him back with you!'

'We could scarcely leave him behind,' Rorke drawled back. 'And since we had to bring him it's better that he calls me Daddy rather than Uncle. I want my father to recover,' he added grimly, 'not suffer another setback.'

'I'll drive you back to Castries.' Helen offered, indicating her car. 'Lisa and Robbie can travel back together with your driver in the Rover.'

Lisa could see Robbie's chin starting to wobble betrayingly. He was a little boy suddenly thrust into a strange environment; over-hot and overtired, and like small children the world over in such circumstances he was about to make it plain that he considered his parents his personal property and wanted them with him, Lisa sensed. She was just about to comfort him when, to her surprise, Rorke stepped forward, sliding into the Range Rover next to the little boy.

'Another time, Helen,' he suggested. 'We'll have to go straight to the hotel anyway, so there's no point in taking you out of your way.'

'Clever of you to foist your child off on him,' Helen hissed as she brushed past Lisa, fury sparkling in her eyes, 'but despite the impression he's giving now, Rorke has never had much time for children—especially another man's!'

'Robbie is Rorke's son,' Lisa told her quietly, 'and nothing either you or Rorke can say can change that, Helen.'

She had the satisfaction of seeing the older woman pale, and knew that her claim had the unmistakable ring of truth.

'You're lying,' Helen accused. 'You left Rorke the day you were married!'

'That doesn't stop Robbie from being his son,' Lisa told her.

'You're just saying that because it's what you want to believe; because it's what you're hoping to force Leigh to believe.?'

'It's the truth,' Lisa insisted. 'You may not want to believe it, but it is.'

Before Helen could make any further response she turned away heading for the Range Rover. Robbie seemed to have recovered his usual good spirits and was staring around, obviously amazed by the sudden change in his surroundings.

It was a long drive down the length of the island from the airport to the hotel near Castries, and

Robbie chattered excitedly, making it unnecessary for Lisa to do much more than stare blindly at the passing scenery. The last time she had made this journey had been the last time she returned from school just after her mother's death. She had travelled with Leigh then, never dreaming what awaited her. In six short months she had grown from a child to a woman, knowing a man's desire, and eventually his contempt. Tears stung her eyes and she blinked them away determinedly, as they turned off the main road and into the drive which led to one of the family's hotels.

In almost no time at all they were shown into one of the hotel's luxurious chalets set in the lush tropical gardens. The chalet was a large one, with two bedrooms, a living room, bathroom and kitchen.

As soon as their baggage had been brought in Lisa started to get Robbie ready for bed. She had bathed him and was just wondering about ordering him something to eat when a beaming maid arrived with a covered tray.

'Master Rorke, he order something for the little boy,' she explained to Lisa when the latter expressed surprise.

'Beans on toast, plus ice cream,' Rorke elucidated, suddenly emerging from the other bedroom. 'Not exactly Cordon Bleu, but I hope it will suffice.'

His thoughtfulness astounded Lisa, but it was swiftly dispelled when he explained mockingly, 'Surely it's only natural that I should show concern for my son's welfare, Lisa? After all, I've already missed the first five years of his life—

thanks to our quarrel. Which reminds me . . .' he added thoughtfully.

Lisa had been settling Robbie with his tray, and she turned at the speculative note in Rorke's voice.

'What?'

'Nothing. I've just got a couple of phone calls to make, that's all. I'll be back in half an hour. Would you like to have dinner in the restaurant, or . . .'

'Here in the bungalow, please, if you can arrange it,' Lisa told him. 'Getting changed for dinner is the last thing I feel like right now.'

'Mmm, I think you're right,' Rorke agreed. 'As we're a newly reconciled couple, it will seem more realistic if we keep to the privacy of our bungalow.'

'We haven't reached St Martin's yet,' Lisa reminded him tartly, 'so it hardly matters what everyone thinks.'

'You seem to have forgotten how parochial these islands are—and how fast news travels,' Rorke reminded her dryly. 'I don't want even the merest suspicion of a cloud to mar Leigh's happiness when he discovers you've come home— and I'll take every step I can to make sure that one doesn't, understand?'

Lisa thought she did, but it wasn't until later—too much later—that she really understood.

Once Robbie was in bed and their clothes laid out for the morning Lisa allowed herself to give in to the full weight of the exhaustion that had been with her since they stepped off the plane. She showered and then sat down in an easy chair, in her robe, intending to read one of the magazines

Rorke had bought her on the plane, but somehow the print kept blurring as waves of tiredness swept over her, and not even the opening of the chalet door had the power to wake her, half an hour later when Rorke returned.

He walked over to the chair, standing over the recumbent feminine form, the flimsy cotton robe doing little to conceal the shapeliness of the curves beneath. With a grim look in his eyes he bent and lifted Lisa into his arms. Her hair fell in a curved silken bell, her body totally relaxed in his arms. With a muttered curse Rorke carried her into the bedroom where a temporary small bed had been set up for Robbie.

'God damn you, Lisa,' he swore softly as he placed her on the bed, 'I let you get to me once, but you're not going to do it again!'

CHAPTER SIX

'MUMMY, wake up! Daddy and I have had our breakfast already!'

She was making a habit of over-sleeping, Lisa thought tiredly, responding automatically to Robbie's voice. Perhaps her body was trying to tell her something—like for instance that dreams were more pleasant than real life.

'Wake up, Lisa, we're leaving in half an hour!'

She opened her eyes, struggling to sit up as she recognised Rorke's voice. Both of them were standing just inside the bedroom door, Robbie leaning against Rorke's legs. Just for a second she allowed herself to imagine that they were in fact the happy family unit they appeared, before firmly reminding herself of the truth. She couldn't bear to look at Rorke again—or Robbie. Seeing them together, Robbie his father all over again in miniature, started off that old familiar weakness she had always experienced in Rorke's presence. She had forgotten over the years the forceful magnetism of his personality, the sheer male force of him, but now, with him standing in the doorway to her room, she found herself trembling with the memory of how she had once felt about him. And it was only memory, she told herself; that was all!

'Lisa.'

She had been so engrossed in her thoughts that the hard edge of impatience in his voice startled her, as did his sudden emergence into her room. He made determinedly for the bed, grasping the bedclothes before she could stop him, Robbie chortling in glee at his side.

'If you aren't going to get up of your own volition, perhaps I ought to help you. Funny, I seem to remember you were always something of an early bird in the old days.'

As he spoke he wrenched back the covers, leaving Lisa feeling ridiculously exposed in her thin cotton nightgown. Robbie, unaware of the friction between the two adults, bounced on the bed beside her, cuddling up to her in a way that reminded her that for all his sturdy independence he still hadn't actually left childhood very far behind.

Having stripped off the bedclothes, Rorke hadn't moved. He simply stood there staring down at them, arms folded across his chest, like a pirate with his human booty, Lisa thought bitterly, and then he moved and just for a moment the expression in his eyes made her heart turn over in sympathy for his anguish. He was watching Robbie, and Lisa stilled an urge to go to him and tell him again that Robbie *was* his son, but she stifled it almost at birth. Rorke wouldn't believe her, if he couldn't believe the evidence of his own eyes. If she told him Robbie was his son he would only think she had some ulterior motive for doing so, and besides, she knew now what the truth would do to him!

'Daddy, why are you looking at me like that?' Robbie piped up, frowning up at Rorke. 'Daddy looks sad, doesn't he, Mummy?' he appealed to Lisa.

Avoiding Rorke's eyes, Lisa said hurriedly, 'Get off the bed, Robbie, there's a good boy, then I can get dressed.'

'Daddy, why are you sad?' Robbie persisted.

Lisa had to walk past Rorke to get to the bathroom and there was no way she could avoid looking at him, surprised to see the tide of dark colour running up under his tan.

'Rorke, is something wrong?' she questioned. She touched his arm as automatically as she might have touched Robbie's in a gesture of comfort and compassion, but Rorke tensed against her, as he might have done a scorpion, and it was her turn to colour heatedly, withdrawing from his obvious rejection.

'Nothing's wrong, Lisa,' he told her grittily. 'You'll just have to make allowances for me occasionally, when I make the mistake of remembering how things should have been—that Robbie should have been my son. He's a fine boy,' he added abruptly. 'A lot like you.'

'He has my eyes,' Lisa replied absently. To judge from Rorke's words it almost sounded as though he regretted their break-up, but he had never to her knowledge made any attempts to trace her or come after her, and surely if he had loved her as she loved him, he would have done so, Mike or no Mike?

'There's very little of Peters about him.' Rorke's voice sounded almost jerky, as though saying the words were a mental and physical agony.

'I think he looks very like his father,' Lisa told him—after all, it was the truth. He did look like Rorke, although the latter couldn't seem to see the resemblance—couldn't or wouldn't, she thought

bitterly. Rorke would never want to acknowledge
Robbie as his son, not when he was so obviously
still involved with Helen. Would he marry her
eventually? Lisa forced herself not to think about
the future. She was back in the Caribbean and for
Robbie's sake she intended to make their time
there a happy one—for Robbie's sake and for
Leigh's as well. Leigh! She had written to him
from London when she first arrived there,
explaining what had happened, but he had never
replied to her. Did he hate her as much as Rorke
had done; did he too believe that Robbie was
Mike's child?

'Peters certainly didn't lose much time in joining
you,' Rorke added tauntingly. 'I saw him before
he left, when I came back from St Lucia without
you. He came to see me; told me that he'd begged
you to tell me the truth. He was most concerned
for you, but not concerned enough to give you his
name, eh, Lisa?—he left that little task to me. Why
did you marry me?'

Robbie was staring at them wide-eyed, taking in
every word, and Lisa glanced pointedly down at
him before responding lightly,

'Oh, all the usual reasons, Rorke. I thought I
loved you, for one thing.'

The bitter anger she saw in his eyes made her
freeze where she stood. 'Liar,' Rorke breathed
harshly. 'You never damned well loved me, Lisa,
otherwise you . . .' He broke off, and Lisa was
amazed to see how pale he had gone beneath his
tan, his face almost grey in the pure morning light.

'You'd better get dressed,' he added coldly,
'otherwise we're going to miss the plane. Having
returned from St Lucia once without you and

faced the consequences, I've no desire to do so again.'

What *had* he said when he returned home without her? Lisa wondered. In the first few weeks after her flight she had been too distressed to give that a thought, and then later she had firmly put her past behind her, refusing to allow herself to think about it, refusing to admit to the pain the memory of Rorke always brought. Why, even now ... She bit her lip. Even now what? Even now she wasn't wholly indifferent to him? Even now her body trembled betrayingly just because he was in the same room? Mere physical response, that was all; that there was nothing left of the love she had once felt for him. There couldn't be!

Nothing had changed, Lisa thought drowsily as she clambered out of the small twin-engined plane and down on to the airstrip of St Martin's. They had flown in over the house, and Lisa now wondered nervously what her reception would be. Had Leigh really been asking for her? If so, why had he never answered her letter? Or was it simply that he had owed more loyalty to Rorke and that now he regretted it?

Even Robbie seemed to be affected by the sombreness of her mood, clinging to her skirt as Rorke talked to the pilot of the plane.

She had changed into a silky cotton two-piece for the last leg of their journey. It was softly patterned in misty blues and lilacs on a white background and Lisa knew it suited her blue eyes and fair colouring. Despite Robbie's birth she was as slender as she had always been, only

the firm fullness of her breasts against the fine
fabric betraying the fact that she was no longer a
girl.

Rorke came to join them and Lisa was
conscious of the pilot eyeing her admiringly.
Fending off unwanted advances was something
she had grown used to in London, and she rarely
bothered even to acknowledge male interest now.
Even so, she was surprised by the icy glint in
Rorke's eyes and the contemptuous way they
raked over her body.

'Just remember you're coming back here as my
wife,' he drawled, grasping her arm in a parody of
an embrace. 'We've just been reconciled, Lisa, with
all that the word implies, and don't you forget it!'

Even then, the full meaning of his words didn't
sink in properly. She was too concerned about the
reception awaiting her at the house; about Leigh's
health and his reaction to Robbie.

She had expected to find Leigh confined to
bed, but the first person she saw as the car drew
up in front of the porticoed entrance was Leigh; an
older, gaunter Leigh, it was true, leaning heavily
on Mama Case's supporting arm, but Leigh
nonetheless, and the tears that had been threatening for so long started to slide helplessly down her
cheeks as she looked through the car window.

Robbie with typical youthful curiosity and lack
of tact chimed brightly, 'Why is Mummy crying?'
drawing Rorke's immediate attention to her
averted profile.

She expected him to make some cynical
comment, and held herself rigid to ward off the
anticipated pain, but instead he said softly, 'I don't
know. Why are you crying, Lisa? It's too late for

regrets now—if you ever had any.' His voice had
taken on a hard note again, and she wasn't
prepared for the warmth of his arm round her
shoulders or the tender concern in his eyes as he
produced a handkerchief and carefully dried her
damp face. Robbie watched the whole proceedings
with round-eyed interest, and Lisa felt the world
around her blur again as fresh tears started. What
was the matter with her? What was she crying for?
Her lost innocence? The love she had once thought
hers? And that tenderness in Rorke's eyes—all
false, of course. They were 'home' now, and they
were reconciled, and he was obviously determined
that she would play her part.

'You could almost be sixteen again.'

The husky warmth of his voice shivered across
her nerve endings and she had to steel herself not
to respond; not to turn into the warmth of his
body and beg him to give her a second chance, to
love her again. Abruptly she dragged her thoughts
to a halt. She didn't want Rorke to love her. She
didn't need his love. What on earth was the matter
with her?

'I know we're supposed to be reconciled, but if
we stay here much longer, they'll be sending out a
search party.'

Rorke eased himself out of the car as he spoke,
coming round to Lisa's side and helping her out.
She thanked him curtly, smoothing the creases out
of her skirt, keeping her eyes on the ground so that
he wouldn't see the fresh tears shimmering there.

'Lisa.'

The touch of his hands on her shoulders
brought her head up. He was standing so close to
her that she could see the texture of his skin, the

scent of his cologne filling her nostrils. His
eyelashes were thick and long, just like Robbie's,
and their deceptive vulnerability tugged at her
heart. The sun was warm on her back, but not as
warm as the lean fingers holding her shoulders. A
sensation of *déjà vu* swept over her, and like
someone in a trance Lisa gazed up at him, aware
that his hand had left her shoulder to sweep up to
her neck, tangling in the softness of her hair, his
lips a mere breath away from her own. She only
had to close her eyes to be in his arms.

'Lisa!'

Was it Rorke who murmured her name, or was
it simply the palms whispering to the wind? The
heat burned into her skin. She touched her tongue
to dry lips, a heated turmoil sweeping through her
body, reality crashing through the dreamlike state
she was in, as she jerked away. But it was too late.
Rorke's fingers slid through her hair, his other
hand sliding down over her spine to rest against
her waist, holding her against the hard masculinity
of his body. He bent his head, and Lisa's eyes
widened, her protest lost beneath the bruising
pressure of his mouth. Dimly she heard a sound
like the surf pounding on the beach and
recognised, in its hypnotic rhythm, Rorke's
heartbeat. Her own sounded more like voodoo
drums pounding out their message. Her entire
body seemed to be on fire, burning with a fever
that left her trembling and weak; too weak to do
anything about Rorke's ravishment of her mouth.

When he released her she felt as helpless as a rag
doll. His touch seemed to have dragged all the
energy out of her. It was as much as she could do
to fix him with a single killing look from eyes that

blazed their defiance, before turning tremblingly towards the car and Robbie.

As she reached for the car door he was behind her, his, 'Welcome home, Lisa,' shivering over too sensitive flesh. She didn't know what was happening to her. She didn't want to know, she thought feverishly, as she helped Robbie from the car. Once down on the ground he said matter-of-factly to Rorke, 'You were kissing my mummy.'

'It's something that mummies and daddies do,' Rorke agreed with an oblique look at Lisah. 'You've seen your mummy being kissed before haven't you?'

Lisa's eyes blazed at him as Robbie shook his head, his little face serious. 'My mummy doesn't kiss anyone but me,' he told Rorke stubbornly, eyeing him for the first time with a hint of doubt, as he added, just in case Rorke had missed the point the first time round, 'She's *my* mummy.'

'How long do you think you're going to be able to hide the truth from him?' Rorke drawled scornfully to her, over Robbie's head. 'Okay now he's young enough to be packed off to bed when you entertain your lovers, but not for much longer, Lisa.'

There was no response she could make without completely losing her temper, and already she could see the anxiety and pain carved deep on Leigh's sunken features. For Leigh's sake she wasn't going to quarrel with Rorke now, but there would come a time of reckoning both for the comment and the insulting way he had kissed her. Kissed her! She bit back a strangled sob; it had been more like rape.

'Lisa!'

There was no mistaking the emotion colouring Leigh's voice, nor the tears shimmering in the dark eyes so like his son's, and grandson's.

'Miss Lisa!' Mama Case echoed, beaming widely. 'You sure am a sight for these old eyes! And who do this be?'

'I'm Robbie,' Robbie supplied importantly, 'and this is my mummy and my daddy.'

'Say hello to your grandson,' Rorke broke in dryly to the emotional silence that followed, adding, 'You got my cable, then?'

'It arrived this morning,' Leigh assured him. He turned to Lisa. 'Lisa, my darling girl, you're everything I always thought you would be. Rorke has made me promise not to ask questions—the past is the past, but you can't know how happy it makes me seeing you both here together, and with your child. I still can't believe it . . .' His voice trailed away, the suspicion of tears moistening his eyes again. Lisa reached out towards him, too full of emotion to speak herself, and it was left to Rorke to supply curtly,

'If the truth were told, I welcomed the excuse of going to find her because you were asking for her, Dad. And once I found her I was determined I wasn't going to let her go again.'

'It must have come as quite a shock to realise you were a father as well,' Leigh chuckled,

'You could say that.' Rorke bent to ruffle Robbie's hair, his expression concealed from Lisa. 'We were going to sail back, but *Lady* had developed engine trouble. Helen met us at St Lucia airport to give us the bad news.'

'Helen?' Leigh's voice and expression sharpened.

'It's all right, Leigh,' Lisa assured him with a

smile. 'Years ago I was jealous of Rorke's relationship with Helen, I know, but I've grown up a lot since then. After all, he married me.'

'And you have his son,' Leigh added emotionally. 'Poor little Lisa, why did you run away like that? It must have been some quarrel the two of you had.'

Lisa frowned. What did Leigh mean? He knew why she had left Rorke—she had written to him.

Mama Case had prepared a celebration lunch for them, and Lisa felt tears sting her eyes as she recognised all her old favourites. Robbie, who could sometimes be a little awkward about his food, tucked in with an enthusiasm that surprised her. Ever since their arrival on the island he had stuck close to Rorke.

After lunch, Leigh announced that he had to go and rest.

'Doctor's orders, I'm afraid,' he grimaced to Lisa. 'Rorke will have told you that they're trying to persuade me to have some damned operation, but it means flying to Florida, and even then there's only a fifty-fifty chance.'

'You know what Doctor James said, Father,' Rorke interrupted. 'First of all you've got to get well enough to have the operation.'

'I sometimes have a rest after lunch,' Robbie piped up, looking at Leigh with interest. He had been quiet during the meal, but now astounded Lisa by saying, 'You're my daddy's daddy, aren't you?'

'Yes, I am,' Leigh agreed gravely, 'and you're my grandson.'

'Are we going to live here for ever?' Robbie asked Lisa, round-eyed.

'I . . .'

'Yes,' Rorke interrupted, frowning her down, and quickly changing the subject. It wasn't fair of him to lie to Robbie. The little boy was too young to understand the reasons behind it and when the day came when they eventually had to leave the island he wouldn't understand. What were Rorke's real intentions? she wondered as she went upstairs with Robbie. Leigh had been looking very tired, and Mama Case explained as she led the way to their rooms that he had only been allowed out of bed because Doctor James had been frightened that he would make himself ill if he didn't agree.

'Him one very sick man,' Mama Case told her, and suppressing a sigh Lisa agreed. Eventually Rorke would have to come to some decision concerning his future. As long as Leigh was so gravely ill she couldn't see him doing anything that would prejudice his father's health, but if Leigh were to have the operation and survive it . . . what then? Would Rorke sue for divorce and marry Helen?

Mama Case stopped outside a bedroom and opened the door.

It was a large room, one Lisa dimly remembered as being empty during her childhood. It was furnished with French Empire furniture, delicate and feminine, festoons of pastel cotton and lace falling from the gilt circlet set in the ceiling above the double bed. The air-conditioning hummed softly, and the French windows were open on to the balcony outside the window.

'The master had this room decorated special for you as a wedding present.' Mama Case explained, adding with a wide smile, 'That sure some quarrel you and Master Rorke have, Miss Lisa. Master Leigh sure was as mad as fire with Rorke when he came back without you. Him say you too young for marriage bed, but not too young to have Rorke's baby, eh?' she concluded with a sly grin at Robbie, who was watching open-mouthed.

Was that what Leigh had thought? Lisa wondered. That Rorke had rushed her into a marriage she wasn't ready for? Had Rorke allowed him to continue thinking that? But what had happened to her letter? It was becoming more and more obvious that Leigh hadn't received it. Could Rorke have kept it from him, preferring to be thought cruel rather than a cuckold? But she had written the truth to Leigh. It was pointless raking up the past now, she thought, suppressing another sigh. For one thing, Leigh's health was too precarious for her to risk upsetting him by dragging up what had happened over five years ago.

'Master Robbie him sleep in here,' Mama Case told her, indicating a room that led off her own room. In it there was a small bed and a chair. The room had obviously once been a dressing room, but it was more than adequate as a bedroom for Robbie and it had the advantage of being close to her. Another door revealed a bathroom decorated in the same colours as her bedroom. Had that too been intended as a wedding present from Leigh? Her heart ached with remembered pain. How had he felt when he learned that she wasn't coming back?

'We'm sure all glad you've come back, missie,' Mama Case said softly. 'Sure as hell missed you, especially the master. When you go it seem you

took all the sunshine with you,' she added softly,
'but you'm back and you'm brought this young
feller with you. He'm all right,' she added,
laughing. 'He'm his daddy all over again!'

With Robbie fast asleep, Lisa prowled tensely
round her room. She ought to be sleeping
herself—she was tired enough, but somehow she
was too restless.

On a sudden impulse she opened her bedroom
door and went downstairs. The entire house
seemed deserted, but then, of course, this was the
time of day when most people slept. Rorke had
always been the exception, she remembered, and
she too had always disdained the siesta period in
those days.

Almost of their own volition her feet trod the
old familiar path down to the cove below the
house. The steps cut in the rock face were
hollowed and worn in places, and Lisa imagined,
as she had always been prone to, those buccaneering ancestors of Rorke's returning to this bay,
climbing these steps, triumphant, their hands full
of the booty they had claimed as they roamed the
Caribbean seas.

The beach was a crescent of soft white sand, and
Lisa gave in to the urge to remove her shoes and
curl her toes into its warmth. The breeze caught
her hair, teasing soft tendrils of it, the surf a soft
lullaby of sound. No one was about, she had the
beach to herself, and suddenly the urge to be once
again the carefree girl she had been five years ago
overwhelmed her. Without giving herself time to
think Lisa pulled off her skirt and top. Her skin
looked almost as pale as the sand, and she
grimaced ruefully, remembering the tan she had

once had. The sea beckoned, and without giving it
a second thought Lisa discarded the lace bra and
briefs she had been wearing under her suit. The
water was warm, like liquid silk, and she struck
out for the reef, swimming strongly, turning to lie
on her back and gaze back at the cove. She had
always enjoyed swimming, preferring the sea to the
pool by the house. There was something about the
Caribbean that no other sea could match. She
remembered a brief holiday she had spent by the
Mediterranean with distaste, recalling the scum
and rubbish tainting the water. Here the sea was
so clean that you could see the bottom, and unlike
the Mediterranean, the islands of the Caribbean
had not been over-developed, nor ever would be.

She would have to swim back to the shore, she
acknowledged, otherwise she was in danger of
falling asleep, lulled by the gentle action of the
waves. Her swim had accomplished what remaining
in her room had not, and now her mind seemed to
be ready for the rest her body craved.

The sand felt hot beneath her damp feet. She
had no towel, and she glanced uncertainly at her
clothes. There was something pagan and wanton
in the stroke of the sun on her body. She had
never swum nude before nor ever wanted to, and
yet now she felt a strange reluctance to return to
the bonds of civilisation. Her skin seemed to crave
the warmth of the sun, drinking it in as though it
had been starved of it for years.

It wouldn't do any harm simply to lie down for
a few minutes and let the sun dry her skin she
decided impulsively, although she would have to
shower once she got back to her room, otherwise
her skin would be sticky and salty.

Robbie! Lisa's eyes flew open, guilt and anxiety filling her mind. She had left Robbie alone! She stretched out a hand for her clothes, stiffening suddenly as she saw Rorke walking towards her, dressed in jeans and a thin cotton shirt open to the waist. She saw his eyes widen fractionally as he took in the exposed curves of her body, and she had to fight against an overwhelming urge to run and hide herself from him. Hot colour seared her skin, and she wished desperately that she had not given in to the childish impulse to swim.

'Well, well, what have we here? You have changed, Lisa,' Rorke drawled, coming to a halt in front of her, his appraisal of her so intimate and thorough that she had to clench her fingers against her palms to stop herself from hitting him. 'It seems to me that I can remember a time when you were too shy even to expose yourself in a swimsuit, and now . . .'

'I came down here on impulse, and decided to swim,' Lisa gritted, fury sparkling in her eyes as she reached for her clothes. 'Turn your back,' she commanded angrily, 'and I'll get dressed. I fell asleep.'

'Yes, Mama Case was getting in quite a panic about you. Just as well that I was the one who remembered how much you used to love this cove, or don't you care any more who sees you naked?'

'Of course I care!' Lisa stormed at him, her fingers trembling as she grasped her clothes. Why on earth didn't he simply go away and leave her in peace? Already her dignity was in shreds. It was like the very worst kind of nightmare, to be exposed and without the protection of clothes while everyone else was fully dressed.

'What were you doing down here in the first place?' Rorke demanded lazily, making no attempt to ease her embarrassment.

'I've told you I was swimming. I came down for some fresh air.'

'Did you, Lisa? Are you sure you didn't remember that I used to swim down here? Are you sure you didn't come down for this?'

She was in his arms, his hands moulding her nakedness against the tautness of his own body, sliding upwards to cup her breasts, his eyes glittering down into her pale face as she fought to deny his claim, but it was like looking at a stranger.

She put out her hands instinctively to fend him off, but it was like trying to stop a steamroller. She could feel the heat coming off his body, burning against her palms despite the cotton shirt between them.

Rorke bent his head, his eyes narrowed against the sun, and instantly her pulses set up a fierce clamorous beat. His mouth touched hers, lightly, tormentingly, and it was like being claimed by the ferocity of the sea pretending calmness while beneath the surface a tempest raged.

She pulled her mouth away from his, shuddering as she fought to free herself from his embrace, hating the sensations his touch aroused as his lips burned hotly against the sensitive skin of her throat, his hands enforcing captivity on her while she struggled helplessly in his arms, hating him with her eyes.

Her anger burned through her in a molten flood, her nails raking protestingly against his back when he refused to release her. She could feel the fierce pounding of his heart, and when he twined his fingers in her hair, pulling her head back sharply so that he could look into her face, she felt the first frisson of fear. The Rorke she knew was barely recognisable in the face above her.

'Rorke, let me go,' she pleaded feverishly, anger forgotten as she recognised the sexual explicitness of his gaze. 'I shouldn't have come down here,' she admitted huskily. 'I'm sorry if I made you angry, but . . .'

'It's too late, Lisa,' he muttered thickly, 'five years too late for apologies. Don't worry, you won't find me any less able than any of your other lovers.'

Lisa felt a growing wave of panic. Rorke was going to make love to her! No, not make love to her—punish her. She bit back a shocked cry as his lips moved lingeringly over her skin, caressing the soft swell of her breast. Panic and pain exploded inside her. Her body felt feverish with a need she wasn't going to admit to. She had to get away before Rorke completely overwhelmed her. She could feel the heat of his fingers against her breast, his thumb teasing the already aroused nipple, his dark hair brushing her skin, as he kept her clamped against him. She tried to push him away again, gasping out loud when he grasped her wrists, pinning them behind her back, exposing her body to the totally male appreciation of his eyes.

His free hand slid slowly over her, and she closed her eyes, unable to bear the cynical mockery in his eyes. What he was doing to her was a parody of everything she had ever wanted from him, and yet her body was responding, she couldn't deny that.

'You're disgusting!' she panted bitterly, trying to use words to hold him off. 'But I suppose it's in your blood. Does Helen know about your depraved tastes; that you like to use force to make women submit to you?'

'Force?' He laughed mockingly. 'Who are you trying to fool, Lisa? Why can't you be honest and admit that you're missing the attentions of your lovers? That's what this is all about, isn't it? Anyone could have walked down here and found you lying there,' he ground out at her, suddenly furiously angry. 'Anyone, Lisa, but I was the one who did, and you can't blame me for taking what you were offering. And as for using force . . .'

His free hand stroked over her breast with a gentleness that made her tense against the need to cry out with pleasure, but her body had already betrayed her, and Rorke knew it. She felt as though her whole body was on fire when his glance dropped to the pale flesh of her breasts, her nipples taut with the desire he had aroused.

Lisa trembled with acute embarrassment, hating the way her body had reacted. What was the matter with her? Just because she had once loved him, just because they had once made love, that was no excuse for her body to turn into helpless trembling wantonness every time he touched it.

'Get dressed, Lisa,' he said tersely, suddenly thrusting her away from him with open bitterness. 'Making love on the beach might be your idea of fun, but I'm long past such adolescent escapades.'

'Oh, I'm sure,' Lisa agreed, bursting into hectic anger as she scrambled into her clothes. 'I'm sure Helen prefers dimmed light, and silk sheets.'

'Be careful,' Rorke warned her, his mouth

thinning, 'otherwise I might start thinking you're jealous!'

Not trusting herself to respond, Lisa pulled on her skirt and top, her cheeks still flushed with anger and embarrassment as she followed Rorke back up to the house. For a moment she thought she caught in his eyes a wild despair that almost brought out of her heart a meek response, but she must have been imagining things, because it certainly wasn't there now.

CHAPTER SEVEN

'But why can't I go to the party?' Robbie pouted, sulking a little.

They were upstairs and Lisa was getting him ready for bed.

'Because it's only for grown-ups,' she explained. Although Robbie didn't know it she would gladly have changed places with him and stayed in bed, instead of attending the small dinner party Leigh had arranged to welcome them home.

Rorke had told her about it after they left the beach. Leigh had invited Doctor James and his lawyer to dinner that evening.

'Do you love my daddy?'

Robbie's voice intruded on her thoughts. He had obviously decided to accept the fact that he couldn't go to the party and was now pursuing another tack.

How on earth could she answer him? Sometimes he surprised her with his astuteness; children always saw so much more than adults wanted to admit they could see. She, for instance, had always told herself that Robbie wouldn't really miss the father he had never known, but she knew now she was wrong. Robbie adored his father and was already patterning himself on him.

'Do you, Mummy?' Robbie persisted. 'Do you love him?'

'Robbie . . .'

'I want to stay with him,' Robbie protested shrilly, anticipating her denial. 'I love him!'

'I love him too.'

How easy it had been to say. Too easy. It was true, she thought numbly, she did still love Rorke! That was why she hadn't wanted to hurt him by forcing on him the myth about Robbie's paternity!

She heard someone turning the door handle, and stiffened instinctively, her eyes mirroring her shock as Rorke walked in. Had he heard her betraying admission? The door was surely too thick for him to have heard anything through it. She looked at him closely, but it was impossible to read anything in his eyes.

'Rorke!' How breathless her voice sounded. 'What do you want?'

His eyebrows rose, the ice-cold blue eyes studying her bleakly.

'It's almost time to get changed for dinner,' he pointed out, starting to unfasten his shirt. Robbie watched him curiously, and seeing the little boy's gaze resting on Rorke's hair-shadowed chest, Lisa anticipated the question hovering on Robbie's open lips and bustled him quickly into his own room.

'I want my daddy to read me a story,' Robbie protested, punishing her promptly. 'Daddy, I want you!'

'This is my room!' Lisa hissed at Rorke as she brushed past him. 'I appreciate that you want to convince everyone that we've been reconciled, but getting undressed in here is taking things a bit far, especially when there's only Robbie and I to see you.'

'Not *your* room, Lisa,' Rorke corrected flatly,

'*our* room. Leigh had it specially decorated for us
before we got married. It was to be a surprise.
When I telephoned from St Lucia and warned
Mama Case that we were bringing Robbie with us
she got this room ready—for both of us.'

'I don't care,' Lisa told him. 'I'm not sharing it
with you!'

'Mummy, you sound cross, 'Robbie murmured
from the bed. 'You're not cross, are you?'

'Of course she's not—are you, Mummy?' Rorke
mocked from Robbie's bed.

She spun round on her heel, closing the door to
Robbie's room behind her. She was not sharing
this room with Rorke, and she was going to make
that plain to him the moment he walked through
the communicating door, and just to make things
easy for him ... She pulled open one of the
wardrobes and found, as she had suspected, that it
was full of Rorke's clothes. Working feverishly,
she started to pile them up on the bed. He could
take them with him when he left. He was still
reading to Robbie, she could hear the even rise
and fall of his voice, and pain throbbed inside her
as though her heartache was a new wound and not
an old one. How often during Robbie's childhood
had she longed for the comfort of Rorke's voice;
of his presence.

The occasions had been too numerous to count.
She could still remember Robbie's birth—vividly.
She had still been hoping against hope even then
that some miracle would occur, that somehow
Rorke and Leigh would be there. She remembered
opening her eyes and finding herself back in a
ward filled with flowers, with happiness and
sunshine, young mothers proudly showing off their

new babies to doting families. Well, she had been a new mother and she had been so proud of her baby son, but there had been no one to show him off to, no one to share the thrill of his birth with.

'Shouldn't you be getting ready?' She hadn't heard Rorke walk in. She watched him glance towards the bed, his mouth tightening in anger as she saw what she had done.

'I'm not sharing this room with you, Rorke,' she told him flatly. 'I mean that.'

'So I see. Why not, I wonder? You're perfectly safe from me, Lisa.'

'Am I? What about when we were down on the beach?'

He shrugged easily. 'So I gave in to a momentary temptation, and you *were* tempting, but I'm over it now. I've reminded myself what you are.'

'And what am I, Rorke?' she demanded bitterly. 'Apart from being your wife and the mother of your son.' She couldn't stop the taunt from rising to her lips.

'Robbie isn't my child. Why do you persist in that lie?'

'Perhaps because it isn't a lie.' She shouldn't have said that. Already she could see Rorke's face beginning to darken.

'Lisa, you know me better than that. Do you honestly think you can convince me that I could forget a thing like making love to you? I thought then you were too young and innocent to see how I felt—how badly I wanted you. I kept away from you deliberately, not wanting to subject you to my desire. I was half ashamed of the way I felt about you,' he muttered, more to himself than her. 'You were so young, almost a child still, and yet very time you looked at me you turned my bones to water. When you touched me I went up in flames. My desire for you was a constant ache that nothing could appease. Now tell me again that I could forget something like making love to you— fully enough to impregnate you with my child. God Lisa!' he swore suddenly, the dark glitter of his eyes frightening her. 'Don't you think I wanted to believe it was my child you were carrying? Don't you think I wanted to believe I was the one who had possessed you, that my kisses had been the ones to stifle your cries of pleasure; that my body had been the one to bring yours to womanhood? But we both know it wasn't. We both know that Mike Peters was your lover, and that he left here to join you shortly after you ran out on me. What I still can't understand is why you bothered marrying me. You must have known that I'd discover the truth, or did you simply hope that my love for Leigh would prevent me from betraying you? That I would uphold the farce of our marriage to protect him? Don't you know yet what your going did to him?'

There was no pity in the dark eyes watching her so mercilessly, wanting to cause her pain.

'Twenty-four hours after I got back here without you, having spent a full day searching St Lucia for you, my father collapsed,' he snarled at her, 'and that's something I can never forgive you for, Lisa. You hurt my father, who loved you as though you were his own child. Perhaps now that you're a mother yourself you can understand just what sort of pain I'm talking about? And you still have the gall to think I want you?' He laughed shortly. 'I brought you here for one reason and one reason alone, Lisa, and it wasn't to share my bed!'

She wasn't going to give in to the pain threatening to storm her frail defences. She wasn't going to plead again for trust and faith from a man who was far too hard and cold to recognise anything other than his own bitter determination to believe the worst of her, who put his faith in his own willpower before anything else.

'I still want you to remove your things from this room,' she managed to enunciate clearly, 'and if you don't, I'll simply call Mama Case and ask her to find someone else to do it.'

She picked up the clothes she had laid out on the bed and marched into the bathroom, locking the door behind her. Once there the frail courage which had kept her from disintegrating in the bedroom drained away completely, leaving her limp and shaking with reaction.

Listening to Rorke, she had almost been able to taste his frustration; his fury that she had eluded him and given herself to someone else—or at least so he thought. Had he ever loved her, really loved her, or was it just as she had feared? He had wanted her, and because of her relationship with Leigh he had married her, only to cast her aside once he discovered what he continued to insist was the truth.

She felt raw with pain, the spirit which had buoyed her up for so long completely disintegrating under the weight of the pain she now suffered. She showered mechanically, salt tears mingling with the cool spray of the water. She had felt she had endured everything there was to endure but she had been wrong. And despite what he said Rorke still wanted her physically. She wasn't seventeen any longer and she had sensed it on the beach this afternoon. He wanted her, no matter how much he might deny it, but it was an ice-cold desire fuelled by a need to punish her for the past—she was sure of that. How long would she have to stay on St Martins? If what Rorke had said about Leigh was true, she daren't risk telling him the truth; the shock might bring on another collapse. Feverishly she towelled herself dry, a momentary glimpse of her pearly flesh in the full length mirrors shocking her into brief stillness. Was it only that afternoon that Rorke had seen her like this? Had touched her?

Unwittingly her hand crept towards her breast as she stifled the cry of pain that knifed through her. She still loved him. It had been sheer madness to think she had ever stopped. Why else had she remained alone all these years, spurning any other male attempts to get closer to her? She loved Rorke. Her shocked, white reflection stared back at her. He must never learn the truth. He would destroy her. She dressed quickly; she had brought only one evening dress with her—she only owned one. She had bought it the previous winter for a party given by the publisher for whom she worked. It was a matt black fabric with shoestring straps and a neckline that hugged the curves of her breasts. The colour suited her, giving her skin a fragile translucence. She pulled it on quickly, checking her reflection in the mirror. She was wearing black silk stockings which might prove uncomfortable in St Martins' tropical climate, but the air-conditioning would help and she had no wish to expose her still pale legs without any covering at all.

She was struggling with her zipper when she heard Rorke rap on the door. 'Hurry up, Lisa,' he demanded. 'I want to shower.'

She opened the door angrily,

'I thought I told you you weren't sharing this room with me,' she told him coldly, glancing at the bed. His clothes were still there.

'Oh, you told me all right,' he agreed sardonically, 'but we happen to have guests for dinner; and I need a shower. I'll see to it later.'

He had removed his shirt completely. His skin was bronzed, the flesh taut over his muscles. Lisa eyed him dry-mouthed, unbearably aware of his male virility and her own reaction to it.

'Very sophisticated,' he mocked, eyeing her dress. 'Quite a change from the demure schoolgirl frocks I remember. You'll cause quite a sensation if you go down like that!'

Too late Lisa remembered that she hadn't closed her zipper.

'Very funny,' she snapped. 'I was just fastening it when you banged on the door.'

'Then perhaps I'd better make amends, and fulfil my husbandly function,' Rorke drawled. His hands gripped her shoulders as she tried to move away, spinning her round so that she could feel his breath fanning the back of her neck.

'Black suits you,' he added.

She tensed automatically as he reached for the zipper, fear exploding inside her as she felt it move down rather than up.

'Rorke . . .'

'There's a thread stuck in it.'

Someone knocked on their door and Lisa felt him stiffen, 'Lisa, Rorke, can I come in?'

It was Leigh. Lisa moistened dry lips, glancing over her shoulder at the clothes lying betrayingly on the bed.

'Don't you dare say a word,' Rorke hissed against her ear. One hand still rested on the bare small of her back, and before Lisa could protest he slipped the other inside her dress, pulling her back against him, so that her back was against his chest, one arm curving possessively round her waist, the other sliding inside the black fabric to cup and caress her breast.

Her sharply explosive protest was silenced as he called out lazily, 'The door isn't locked—come on in.'

As the door opened he lowered his head to her shoulder, his lips against the creamy flesh. Leigh walked in and Rorke withdrew his hand from her dress, but so slowly that Leigh couldn't have been in the slightest doubt about what he was doing. Lisa flushed bright red, but Rorke only looked amused.

'We're supposed to be getting ready for dinner,' he told his father lazily, 'but seeing Lisa in that dress reminded me that I had other appetites and that it's been a long, long time since I last indulged them.'

'You're embarrassing Lisa,' his father protested, but he too was smiling, until he looked at the bed and saw the clothes piled on to it.

'Just like a woman,' Rorke drawled again. 'Lisa took it into her head to start rearranging the cupboards. She seems to think that Mama Case has given me the lion's share. Which, of course, is only right and proper and just as it should be!'

'How's Robbie,' Leigh asked, obviously deceived by Rorke's easy explanation.' 'Has he settled down all right?'

'To the manner born,' Rorke replied for her,

'I'm so glad you came back, Lisa,' Leigh told her.

'I'm so glad you want me back.'

Her voice was thick with tears, but she couldn't pretend with Leigh. She had missed him dreadfully, and her bitterness against Rorke had been increased by the fact that she had been deprived of a father as well as a lover.

'Oh, my darling girl, how could you ever think that we didn't? Is that what you thought, Lisa?'

'I . . .' She moistened her lips. If only Rorke wasn't here and she could speak freely!

'It's over,' Rorke interrupted. 'And I for one don't want to be reminded of the time Lisa spent away from me.'

There was a look in his eyes which reminded Lisa of her earlier conviction that he still wanted her physically.

'I'll go down with Leigh,' she said hastily. 'We'll leave you to get dressed in peace.'

'Spoilsport—but aren't you forgetting something, darling?'

His hand slid down her naked back, tracing the shape of her spine, his free arm imprisoning her so that there was no way she could escape the tormenting caress.

'I can see when I'm not wanted!' Leigh chuckled, making for the door. 'We'll talk together later, honey,' he said to Lisa.

'One word, just one word to make him think that we're not blissfully reconciled and I'll make you sorry you were ever born!' Rorke threatened when the door closed behind his father.

'You've already done that,' Lisa sniped back at him, pulling away. 'And anyway, I wouldn't dream of hurting Leigh. He means a great deal to me.'

'Oh, sure,' Rorke agreed cynically, 'so much that you simply walked out on him without so much as a word!'

'I wrote him a letter,' Lisa protested, but Rorke brushed aside her claim, anger chilling his eyes as he surveyed her flushed cheeks and tangled hair.

'You look innocent enough,' he muttered beneath his breath, 'but we both know how deceptive appearances can be, don't we, Lisa? Just tell me one thing,' he was breathing harshly, and she could see the tension in his muscles as he crossed the room and came towards her. 'If I hadn't taxed you with the truth would you have let me make love to you?'

'Why not?' she threw at him wildly, 'I'd married you hadn't I?'

'And Peters didn't mind?'

'Why should he?' Lisa retorted coolly. 'Mike knew the truth.'

'He couldn't have thought very much of you, Lisa, if he let you leave his arms for mine—but then we both know that he didn't, don't we? Otherwise he would have married you.'

'You're despicable, Rorke!' Lisa told him, choking out the words. 'You measure everyone by your own standards and because of that you can't recognise the truth when you hear it. You were my only lover, Robbie is your child.'

'I'll give you ten out of ten for persistence

anyway,' he muttered as he thrust past her. 'What are you hoping to do, Lisa? Wear me down by constant repetition? It can't have been easy bringing him up on your own, despite the help I'm sure you've received over the years from your lovers. Perhaps you're just beginning to realise that marriage does have its compensations after all, mm? You shouldn't have run out on me.'

'You didn't give me much option, as I recall,' Lisa retorted coldly. 'And now, if you'll excuse me, I want to finish getting dressed.'

'Feel free.' His bored glance slid over her exposed skin. 'That's a very sexy dress, Lisa, as I'm sure you know, but when I remember what lies under your undoubtedly alluring skin, somehow it turns me off.'

Lisa heard his whistling as he turned on the shower. Her fingers were trembling as she pulled up her zipper and put on her make-up. She checked quickly on Robbie before putting on her shoes. The little boy was fast asleep. She was still trembling with a mixture of anger, and something she was forced to admit could only be thwarted desire when she went downstairs.

She found Leigh in the drawing room—alone.

'Ah, Lisa, my dear, you look lovely,' he complimented her as she kissed his cheek. 'Where's Rorke?'

'Still getting ready.'

'And you didn't wait for him because you knew it was only likely to delay him even more,' Leigh teased. 'Oh, my dear,' he continued emotively, 'I can't tell you what it means to have you back here, to see you reconciled with Rorke. And Robbie— an added bonus for a man who thought he'd never live to see his grandchildren. Lisa, why didn't you write to us, tell us that you were safe at least? Rorke nearly went out of his mind! He searched the length and breadth of St Lucia for you before he discovered that you'd flown to England. He went after you, but he couldn't trace you.'

He wouldn't have been able to, Lisa acknowledged. She had changed her name, booking into a small boarding house that didn't worry about such formalities as seeing passports, and she had paid cash, using some of the money she had changed at the airport. Then, she had been too bitterly hurt to care whether Rorke came after her or not, and then, later when she did care, it had been too late.

'You never touched your allowance,' Leigh reproached. 'You never even told us about Robbie.'

'I wrote to you,' Lisa told him. 'My letter must have gone astray. I wanted you to know about Robbie—about what had happened.' Her voice broke, tears flooding her eyes. Dear God, she mustn't cry now, but it was too late, Leigh had seen her tears and she was in his arms. It frightened her to realise how frail he had become, and to think that she might in some part be responsible.

'Your letter never reached us,' he told her. 'I was worried about you. I blamed myself for what happened. I could see how much Rorke wanted you. It was obvious from the way he looked at you, and just as obvious that he was fighting against it. He avoided being alone with you, but I loved you both so much, Lisa, and selfishly I wanted to keep you with me. I threw you both together. Rorke wanted you intensely, I could see that, and although you were so young I knew you cared for him.' He sighed. 'What I did was wrong, as Rorke has so often told me. You were a child, and Rorke was a fully grown man, it was inevitable, I suppose . . . He had restrained himself too much before the wedding . . . my fault again. Had you not been living here under my protection . . .'

'He would simply have indulged in an affair with me and that would have been that,' Lisa supplied dryly. 'Oh, I have no illusions, Leigh,' she continued honestly. 'Rorke might have wanted me. . . .'

'Too much, perhaps,' Leigh interrupted sadly. 'and because of that; because he had been forced to keep his feelings on such a tight rein, he frightened you and you ran away.'

'He told you that?' Lisa was amazed.

Leigh shrugged, 'Not in so many words. He didn't need to. I taxed him with it when he returned without you, and he didn't deny it. It must have come as quite a shock to you to discover you were having his child. Didn't you even think of coming home then, Lisa?'

'Many times,' she agreed honestly, 'but somehow I just couldn't.'

'No, you always were a proud little thing. But you're back now, and I can't tell you how much it means to me.'

'Does it mean enough for you to have your operation?' Rorke asked quietly from the door. Neither of them had heard him enter and they both spun round like guilty children.

'Rorke, I'm too tired and too old,' Leigh protested. 'What can a few more years of life mean to me now?'

'A great deal, I should think. In five years Robbie will change from a little boy to a growing adult. In ten he'll be fifteen. And perhaps there'll be other children.' He crossed the room and took Lisa in his arms, a teasing glint lightening the darkness of his eyes.

'If I'm so successful at parenthood without even trying, think what I might be able to achieve if I do try! Aren't there twins somewhere along the line in the family?' he mused as Lisa bit back a protest. Her knees had gone strangely weak, her senses bemused by Rorke's proximity. He had changed into formal dinner clothes and just for a moment she was tempted to ruffle the tidiness of his hair, to slide her fingers inside the crisp whiteness of his dress shirt. He was dangerous in this teasing mood. Against her will she could feel herself responding to him; wanting him, only this time without a teenager's natural fear and apprehension.

'I don't know,' Leigh was saying, but there was enough doubt in his voice for Rorke to glance triumphantly at Lisa, and say lightly, 'Well let's put it to Doctor James, shall we?'

Dinner was a surprisingly pleasant meal. David Neale she knew from the past, and he had always been someone she liked, despite the fact that he was Helen's uncle, and neither of their guests made any reference to the past, or Lisa's unexpected reappearance, which made it easy for her to behave naturally.

Doctor James, of course, she didn't know, but he was a pleasant, sturdy Scot with a dry sense of humour and an obvious concern for his patient.

'Rorke's been on at me again to have that

operation,' Leigh commented abruptly during the course of the meal. Lisa looked queryingly at the doctor, wondering what his response would be.

'Well, you know my views,' Doctor James responded. 'Life is always precious enough to risk hanging on to it. You have a fifty-fifty chance of coming through the operation—more if you continue to make the same progress you've been doing lately. You've been a real tonic to him,' he told Lisa. 'Far better than any of my pills and potions.'

'Well, Lisa, what do you think?' asked Leigh.

'Perhaps I'm being selfish, in saying this, but I'm all for anything that keeps you with us Leigh, you know that.'

'It looks very much as though I'm overruled,' Leigh commented wryly, but Lisa could tell that he wasn't entirely displeased. She even had a suspicion that he had already decided in favour of the operation anyway. Leigh had always been astute, and clever. Could he possibly have persuaded Doctor James to tell Rorke his health was worse than it was, in a bid to force Rorke to take her back? Leigh loved her, Lisa knew that. He also held marriage to be sacrosanct. He had fully accepted Robbie as his grandson, and for the first time Lisa faced the fact that if Leigh did have the operation, if he did recover, she and Rorke would be sentenced to a lifetime of misery together. But Rorke was his father all over again. He would never allow himself to be forced into any situation he didn't want, at least not for long, and no doubt he already knew exactly what he was going to do to extricate himself from their marriage.

One of the servants had just brought in the

cheeseboard and a decanter of port, when Leigh signalled to him, murmuring something Lisa could not quite catch. The man beamed and hurried to the door, flinging it open to reveal Mama Case and the rest of the household.

'Rorke, if you would do the honours.' Leigh indicated several magnums of champagne on the trolley. 'I bought this the year you were born, and I kept some of it to celebrate the birth of your first son. Unfortunately that was an event we missed.' He sighed, and Lisa coloured guiltily, telling herself that really she had nothing to feel guilty for.

'I want you all to drink with me now—not just Robbie, my grandson, but to Lisa and Rorke, his parents. May they always find their happiness in one another.'

Everyone drank but Lisa found it hard to look suitably happy.

'There's something else.'

Lisa could see the hectic colour staining Leigh's pale face and she could tell that Rorke shared her concern. Too much excitement wasn't good for him, he had told her.

'As you all know, up until now Rorke has always been my heir. Events such as those I've lived through recently make a man all too aware of his mortality, and one of the reasons I've asked you to come here tonight is that I want you all to know that I've rewritten my will. The bulk of my estate—the management of the hotels still goes to Rorke, but ownership of the hotels he now shares with his son—Robbie is still far too young for such a responsibility, and so his mother will act for him until he comes of age.'

An excited buzz of chatter broke out all around her, but Lisa barely heard it. What had Leigh done? Did he suspect that they were simply acting? Was this his way of ensuring that they were forced to stay together, or was it simply that he wanted to do something for Robbie, sensing perhaps that Rorke did not fully accept the little boy.

She darted a glance at Rorke. He could not have known what his father had planned. His face was white with tension, his eyes hard as they met hers. He hadn't known. Her heart started to beat erratically. Did he blame her? Did he think she had persuaded Leigh to alter his will?

'Rorke, I can't let your father do this,' she said shakily. 'I . . .'

'Don't say a word,' Rorke warned her. 'He thinks he's pleasing you, Lisa, don't spoil his pleasure. Do you want him to have another relapse? Look at him,' he demanded harshly. 'He isn't well, Lisa. All that's keeping him going is sheer guts and strength of will. He knows you too well. He's frightened that you might run off again, so this time he's keeping you tied here. You think too much of Robbie to deny the boy his inheritance.'

'And you don't mind?'

He shrugged. 'Why should I? There's plenty to go round.'

Half an hour later Doctor James suggested in a quiet aside to Lisa that it might be as well to bring the evening to a close.

'He's doing marvellously well, but he's still very frail. Having you and the boy here has given him a new lease of life. By the way,' he added thoughtfully, 'you might as well bring the laddie down to the hospital one of these days. I take it he's had all his inoculations?'

'Most of them,' Lisa agreed, 'but there wasn't time to have them all done before we left.'

'Well, bring him down to see me,' Doctor James reminded her, as he went to take his leave of his host.

She had forgotten about Robbie's booster injections in the panic of leaving England in such a hurry and was glad that Doctor James had reminded her. St Martins was, fortunately, free of tropical diseases, but it still wouldn't hurt for him to have some form of protection. She had been remiss in not arranging for it herself, Lisa acknowledged.

'You're looking extremely thoughtful. Worrying about the responsibility of looking after Robbie's inheritance, are you?'

Lisa glared at Rorke. He had materialised at her side unexpectedly, his arm curving round her waist as though to proclaim their intimacy.

'No, Dr James has just reminded me that Robbie needs to have some injections. I'd completely forgotten about it.'

'And now you're suffering from maternal pangs of guilt. You're very protective of your child, Lisa.'

'Perhaps because he's all I've got,' she responded hotly.

'Whose fault is that? Have you tried reminding his father of his responsibilities towards him? I should have thought Peters would be proud to acknowledge Robbie as his son. He's a fine boy, Lisa.'

Was it her imagination or had his voice softened

slightly? It gave her no satisfaction to know that Rorke was talking about his own child; trying to get the truth through to him was like beating her head against a brick wall, and she was tired of trying.

She disengaged herself, pushing away his arm, and went over to where Leigh was talking to David Neale.

'Ah, Lisa, my dear, I'm just on the point of leaving,' the lawyer said with a smile. 'It's wonderful to see you back here. I'm glad you and Rorke were able to resolve your differences.'

He was, but his niece didn't share his feelings, Lisa thought bitterly, but then Helen knew the truth, and no doubt wasn't worried in the slightest about Lisa's presence in Rorke's life.

'I was just telling him he must come down and see Robbie,' Leigh added. 'He's the image of Rorke at that age,' he added to David Neale. 'But unlike Rorke he's fortunate in having a devoted mother. Elise didn't really want children, and she always kept Rorke at a distance. He sensed it too. I remember whenever he fell over or hurt himself he would never cry in Elise's presence, nor would he ever go voluntarily to her.' He sighed. 'It all seems such a long time ago now. Elise and I should never have married. Unlike you and Rorke, my dear,' he said to Lisa. 'You were made for one another. There's only one thing I want now . . .'

'Oh, what's that?' Rorke demanded, joining them at the tail end of the conversation.

'A granddaughter who looks as much like her mother as my grandson does his father,' Leigh told him simply.

'Lisa forced herself to join in the general

laughter that followed Leigh's comment, allowing Rorke to put his arm round her waist as they walked with their guests to the front door.

Rorke slipped away when Leigh and Lisa turned back from the door, and Lisa presumed he had gone to make arrangements to transfer his things into another room. She didn't care what conclusions the staff drew, she was not sharing a room with him. He could make what excuses he liked!

'Come and talk to me, Lisa,' Leigh insisted as she headed for the stairs. 'We haven't talked properly since you arrived.'

'I'm under pain of death or worse from Rorke if I overtire you,' she responded lightly.

'You are glad to be back, aren't you, Lisa? Sometimes you look very sad.'

'Only because I'm thinking of all the wasted years.' How glibly the lies slid off her tongue!

'That's behind you now. We never knew about Robbie,' he said emotively, 'Lisa, why didn't you tell us?'

Rorke knew, she wanted to protest, Rorke knew and denied him.

'I did,' she said shakily instead, 'I wrote to you—remember I told you earlier and when you didn't reply I thought . . . I thought . . .'

'You thought we'd turned our backs on you. Oh, Lisa, how could you think that? Rorke is a proud man, I know, and you hurt him badly, but surely you never imagined that he wouldn't welcome you back with open arms, especially when . . .'

'When I'd given birth to his son?' How could she tell Leigh that Rorke had known and that because of that knowledge he had rejected both her and Robbie? She couldn't!

Wearily she followed Leigh upstairs. The evening had been a traumatic one in many ways. Time enough tomorrow to worry about how she was going to deal with the bombshell Leigh had dropped about his will.

In many ways she could understand his determination to keep them together—after all, wasn't that really what she wanted? To be Rorke's wife; to be loved and cherished as his lover and the mother of his children? Only that was never likely to happen. Rorke despised her. He had made that more than plain.

She pushed open the bedroom door, coming to an abrupt halt as she saw the lean, indolent figure propped up against the wall.

CHAPTER EIGHT

'RORKE! I thought I told you I wasn't going to share this room with you,' she said bitterly.

'So you did,' he agreed blandly, extracting a key from his pocket and deftly locking the door behind her before returning the key to his pocket. 'And I told you that I wasn't going to allow you to worry my father any more than you have done already. We've been reconciled, Lisa, remember? He knows how much I wanted you before, no way is he going to believe that wanting you like that I'm going to allow you to sleep in another room.'

'I'm not sleeping in this room with you!' Lisa protested fiercely, her eyes going to the bed. His clothes had been removed. Where had he put them? Back into the wardrobe? 'There was nothing in our arrangement about this, Rorke.'

'Oh, come on,' he drawled cynically. 'Think what you're getting out of all this, Lisa. Is it so much to ask? That you simply allow my father to believe we're idyllically happy together? Just think of what you're getting in return. Security for you and for Robbie. It's a damn sight more than either of you got from his father!'

The sound of her open palm against his face shocked her. She hadn't meant to hit him, but somehow it had been the only way to alleviate the rage boiling up inside her.

'Bitch!' Rorke muttered thickly, touching the place where her hand had left a scarlet imprint against his skin. 'What's the matter, Lisa, don't you like being reminded of Peters? I should have thought his son was a constant reminder.'

'Robbie is your son!' Lisa hurled at him. 'Are you blind? Can't you see that he's the image of you? Everyone else can.'

'Everyone else sees what they want to see, but I know the truth. And don't tell me again that I made love to you on board *Lady* . . .'

'Why not?' Lisa demanded bitterly. 'It's the truth . . ,' suddenly too enraged to want to protect him any longer.

'It can't be. I promised myself I wouldn't touch you until we were married, I . . .'

'You were suffering from concussion, although I didn't realise it properly, and you *did* make love to me, Rorke.'

'No!' He was breathing heavily, his eyes glittering with a mixture of emotions, and not for the first time Lisa realised how bitterly he would have fought against possessing her before they were married. Although she hadn't realised it at the time, he had kept a tight rein on his feelings. That night in St Lucia had been the first time she had realised he wanted her. He had had no intentions of making love to her; they had even had separate cabins, but somehow his accident had caused him to push aside his self-imposed restraint and he had possessed her—fiercely and intensely, Lisa remembered, almost frightening her with the depth of his passion. Was that why he refused to remember what had happened between them? Wouldn't his mind allow him to acknowledge that he had weakened; had done what he had sworn not to? She sighed.

'Admit it, Lisa,' he said huskily. 'Admit that I never touched you that night.'

'Why?' she demanded tautly. 'Why should I?'

'Because every time you throw it at me, it's a physical torment. I can't believe that I could touch you and not remember . . . I can't believe that . . .'

'That's your problem, not mine, Rorke,' Lisa taunted him. She was enjoying getting under his skin, enjoying the tension building up inside him. Was he actually beginning to doubt himself? If so she was glad. Let him suffer as she had suffered!

'And anyway, if you really believe you never touched me why did you let Leigh acknowledge Robbie as his grandson?'

'Just what the hell are you trying to imply?'

His fingers dug into her shoulders and she cried out in protest, but he refused to set her free. 'Robbie isn't my child, Lisa, but perhaps I'd be a fool not to take what I can from this damnable situation and make sure the next one is.'

'No!'

The denial was torn from a dry throat. Lisa tried to pull away from him, but his fingers bit cruelly into her tender skin. 'No, Rorke,' she protested, reading the intent in his eyes. 'You said you wouldn't touch me . . .'

'Ah, but you want me too, Lisa.'

It was said so dulcetly that at first she thought she must have misheard him, but his fingers were already sliding under the straps of her dress, easing it from her shoulders. The single lamp cast mellow shadows across her skin, and Lisa felt Rorke expel his breath slowly, as he bent his head and touched his lips to the smooth skin of her shoulder.

Her pulses raced frantically, the effort of containing her breathing to even calmness torturing her aching lungs. Whatever happened she mustn't let Rorke see how he affected her. She kept perfectly still as his lips moved tormentingly across her skin. She felt him reach behind her, the musky, male scent of his body enveloping her as he found her zipper and slid it down. She wasn't going to plead with him. That was what he wanted. He wanted her to beg him to stop, but she wasn't going to. Her stomach muscles ached with the effort of fighting down the sensations spreading through her. Her arms were rigid at her sides, and she could feel her dress slipping downwards. Rorke's fingers caressed her spine, tracing the vertebrae and sending shivers of pleasure coursing through her. She could feel the silkiness of his shirt against her breasts and felt a primitive longing for the intimate caress of flesh against flesh.

'You're a very desirable woman, Lisa,' Rorke murmured into her throat, 'far more desirable now than you were at seventeen. There's an allure about you, curiously at odds with your maternal state, an almost virginal aloofness. It must drive your lovers wild to possess you, to make you ache with the need that consumes them.'

Lisa shivered with the intimacy of his words; the pictures unwillingly conjured up by her feverish mind. Rorke had been her only lover and already she yearned for his touch.

'Why aren't you touching me, Lisa?' he murmured against her skin. 'I know you want to.'

'I don't,' she protested, forced to make the curt denial, but his hands were already cupping her breasts, his thumbs stroking tauntingly over the aroused nipples. Her flesh seemed to swell at his touch, wantonly seeking his possession, no matter how much she tried to shrink away.

'Liar,' he drawled sardonically, looking down into her eyes. 'Perhaps the most effective punishment for your crimes would be for me to arouse in you the need you once aroused in me, Lisa. For you to endure the agonising ache of wanting that eats into you, never allowing you a moment's peace. Have you ever wanted anyone like that?'

She said nothing. He was the only man she had ever wanted, but it had been an adolescent's wanting. After Robbie's birth she had closed her heart and mind against physical desire. She had Robbie to worry about, and he filled her life. She wanted to plead with Rorke to set her free, not to subject her to such humiliation, but deep down inside her she recognised that there was a need in him to punish her as he had described. Perhaps he had never stopped resenting the fact that he wanted her; even though it was now in the past. Perhaps the very fact that he had once done so was a permanent scar on his pride.

He moved and her dress slithered to the floor, leaving her dressed only in black silk French knickers and her silk stockings and suspender belt. Her embarrassment was as unfeigned as Rorke's very obvious and totally masculine appreciation.

'You have changed, Lisa,' he remarked softly. 'At seventeen you wouldn't have had anything like that in your wardrobe, never mind worn it. Once I thought I was going to be the man who taught you how to give and take pleasure, but obviously I was wrong. However, someone has taught you, and I'm most appreciative.'

Tension locked her throat. He might say he was appreciative, but he certainly didn't sound it, nor after that one illuminating glance did he look it. In fact he looked furiously angry, and Lisa was angry too. It was an insult to suggest that she had dressed with deliberate sensuality. She had simply worn the underclothes she always wore under that particular dress. At home she might have worn tights, here she had worn stockings simply because they were cooler; but something told her that even if she explained to him Rorke wouldn't believe her.

His hands moved to her hips and she stiffened as she felt the warmth of his fingers against her skin, deftly removing her stockings. He picked her up as easily as he might have done Robbie, carrying her over to the bed and placing her on it, trapping her against the coverlet with his arms either side of her body. She knew that he was going to kiss her and she told herself that she could resist him, but the kisses she remembered had been tempered to her youth, and the mouth closing on her own wouldn't let her resist. She tried to keep her lips tightly pressed together, but Rorke nipped her with his teeth, making her gasp with the brief pain, allowing him to devour the moist sweetness she had withheld from him, and Lisa felt her senses sliding out of control. Her arms clung weakly to his shoulders, her fingers finding and unfastening the buttons of his shirt, her palms pressing urgently against the moist warmth of his chest.

She strained upwards automatically to meet the pressure of his kiss, barely aware of the fact that he was slowly drawing away from her, forcing her to cling urgently to him to prolong the kiss.

She felt the bed give way as he joined her on it, quivering under the sensual stroke of his fingers over her hips and across her stomach before he untied the silk ribbon fastening of her French knickers. Lisa stared at him helplessly as he removed the last barrier of her clothing, shivering as his fingers curled round her ankle, to stroke slowly upwards, caressing the long curve of her thigh. An explosive tension built up inside her, sensations she could barely remember springing to life. Had she felt like this that first time? Had she experienced that same wanton need to touch his body as he was touching hers? This was what he wanted, she acknowledged as a hot tide of desire flooded through her. He wanted her to feel like this, to want him. His lips caressed her throat and she moaned softly with pleasure, the last tautly straining vestiges of control snapping under his skilled assault on her senses. No longer caring what he might think, she buried her hot face against his skin, letting her lips taste the warm saltiness of his flesh, barely aware of the fact that he was shrugging out of his shirt with muttered impatience, until she felt the burning warmth of his chest against the aroused sensitivity of her breasts.

His lips stroked slowly over her throat, encouraged on their downward path by the instinctive arching of her body. Her heartbeat thudded like jungle drums as Rorke lifted her towards him, his tongue and lips teasing first one erect nipple and then the other, as Lisa pressed herself against him in a frenzy of need, brief, inarticulate murmurs of pleasure escaping her lips, her fingers locking in his hair, trying to prolong the pleasure he was giving her. It no longer mattered that she was betraying to him how much she wanted him; she was past caring what she betrayed. Her entire world was encapsulated in the sensations centred deep inside her, the age-old primitive need for possession; Rorke's possession.

Her overheated flesh seemed to burn with longing for his touch. Lisa was barely aware of scattering wild kisses against his shoulders and throat as she clung to him, rapidly becoming aware that her desire wasn't all one-sided. Rorke wanted her too, and no matter how much he might try to deny it his body betrayed him as hers did her.

She moaned softly, enjoying the pleasure of feeling the weight of his body on hers; the tautness of his thighs and his very evident desire.

'I've wanted this for years, dreamed of it and ached for it,' he muttered thickly as his hands investigated the curves of her hips. Her own need was a physical ache inside her, and Lisa couldn't believe it when he slowly released her and got off the bed, her eyes betraying the emotions that quickened her sensitive flesh.

'It hurts, doesn't it, Lisa?' he mocked her, crouching down beside her, and grasping her chin so that she was forced to look into his eyes. 'Ah, yes, I can see it does. You want me, and we both know it.' His fingers stroked lazily down the length of her body and she shivered and trembled visibly under the languid caress.

'Well, I'm not going to torment you as you tormented me, Lisa. All you have to do is ask, that's all.'

He was watching her with cruelty in his eyes, and she summoned every ounce of willpower she had to defy him. She wasn't going to give in; she wasn't going to pander to his massive ego, and she would tell him so.

'Rorke.'

Strange how weak and shaky her voice sounded. Not at all as she had intended it to do.

'Lisa,' he mocked softly.

'Rorke . . .' She looked into his face and was suddenly overwhelmed by a flood of love and need that made her very bones ache. 'Rorke, I want you—I need you.' She heard herself crying like a child in pain, the sound of her own anguish tormenting her, so that tears filled her eyes and rolled helplessly down her cheeks, as she turned her head aside, expecting with every breath Rorke's rejection and scorn. She knew he had moved away from the bed, and bitterly regretted her weakness. Why had she given in so easily? Because she loved him and some deeply primitive instinct urged her to capitulate so that they met on the only common ground they still had; their mutual desire. But obviously Rorke's desire had been satisfied by her abasement. He no longer wanted her, her humiliation had all been for nothing, he . . . She tensed as she felt the warm brush of his mouth against her damp skin. Fresh tears flowed, and kept on flowing in soundless agony until Rorke stopped the flood with the kisses he placed against her closed lids.

'Don't cry, Lisa,' he murmured against her skin. 'Don't cry, everything's going to be all right.' His hands were gentle on her skin. There was no haste, no urgency, and it came to Lisa on a sudden rush of knowledge that this was the wedding night they had never had. Her admission that she wanted him had, temporarily at least, satisfied the devils that drove him, and he was obviously prepared to be generous in victory.

'You're more beautiful than I ever imagined,' he murmured huskily against her skin. 'More perfectly feminine than I thought possible.'

He moved, and moonlight glinted over his body, and Lisa realised that he too was naked, his body as perfectly sculptured as she remembered. His hands left her body and she trembled, thinking that he meant to leave her now when her mind and body were at their most vulnerable with wanting him, but instead she felt the warmth of his lips against her instep gradually moving upwards, his hands and lips caressing her body until she thought she could no longer bear the waves of desire pounding through her. She shuddered helplessly beneath his touch, whispering pleas he would only ignore, apparently intent only on giving her the utmost pleasure—pleasure so intense it was almost a pain. The touch of his mouth against her thigh made her cry out with the exquisite agony of wanting him, her incoherent protests suddenly smothered beneath the pressure of his lips as his own need drove out his earlier gentleness and he held her against the length of his body, hard and urgent with desire, his kisses drowning out everything but the need he was feeding with his hands and his mouth.

'Lisa, Lisa . . .' he murmured her name like an incantation between kisses, parting her thighs almost roughly, possessing her mouth in a long deep kiss as his control snapped beneath the weight of his desire, and the savage imprecation he muttered beneath his breath was lost on the rising storm that swept them both.

It was nothing like it had been the first time. Surprisingly there was pain and she felt his stilled response to it; and then pain and every other consideration was swept aside in the swirling molten force clamouring for appeasement, and she remembered nothing except crying out Rorke's name as she plunged with him into a deep pit of golden darkness. As she lay exhausted on the fringe of sleep she thought she heard Rorke murmur her name and she fought valiantly to respond—to assure him now, when surely he would believe her, that she was his and his alone. But the words slipped away before she could utter them.

What on earth was that noise? Someone was banging on the door. Lisa opened her eyes and fought for consciousness. Robbie—something was wrong with Robbie! But no, Robbie was there standing beside her, eyeing her with round-eyed disapproval.

'You haven't got any clothes on,' he pronounced at last, adding, 'and neither have you, Daddy.'

Daddy! Lisa froze. Rorke was in bed—with her? The events of the previous evening came flooding back. She couldn't bear to look at Rorke. What on earth must he think of her, or was he enjoying his victory too much to think about her at all?

'I suppose I'd better go and open that door.' She felt the bed give as he got up, pulling on a towelling robe that had been lying on a chair. 'Okay, okay,' he called lazily as he found the key and unlocked the door. 'What's all the hurry?'

'All the hurry be that this here coffee be getting cold,' Mama Case scolded as she waddled into the room with a breakfast tray, her face breaking into a wide beam as she drew her own—and obvious—

conclusions from the untidy disarray of the room and Lisa's hot face.

'No need to blush, honey,' she chortled to Lisa. 'You'm a married lady right enough, and you've got the marriage lines to prove it.'

'What were you doing in bed with my mummy?' Robbie demanded accusingly,

'Mummies and daddies always share beds, honey chile,' Mama Case told him with a grin, winking at Rorke. 'I think it's time we found this young man a room of his own somewheres.'

'Oh no,' Lisa protested instinctively. 'He's always shared with me . . .'

'Then he'm gonna have to get used to not doing,' Mama Case retorted firmly. 'Especially when you've got another little one to attend to——'

She had forgotten how earthy the islanders could be, Lisa reflected as Robbie protested and came back to the bed, climbing on to it and snuggling up to her. She had never made a particular thing about concealing her body from Robbie, but then neither had she deliberately drawn attention to her nakedness. She wanted Robbie to accept the differences between male and female naturally, but believed that, as yet, he was far too young to do so. He was already reaching the stage where he sometimes preferred privacy when he was undressing, and Lisa had wisely respected this need. However, when he pulled aside the bedclothes and snuggled up to her, she made no attempt to stop him. Robbie often came into bed with her at weekends for a special cuddle, and although admittedly she was always wearing a nightgown, she sensed that to reject him now because she was not would be something he wouldn't understand. Robbie was, after all, only a little boy, and yet the dark head against her breast was far too reminiscent of his father's not to be disturbing, and as Robbie dislodged the sheet she was intensely aware of Rorke's eyes on her body. Her muscles tensed in remembered desire as she trembled with the memory of her wanton response to him.

'Robbie—out,' Rorke commanded curtly, while Lisa looked at him in surprise. He had never spoken so firmly to the little boy before, and even more surprisingly Robbie responded to him, sliding sulkily out of the bed and running across to Mama Case.

'That Rorke, he think there is only room for one male in your bed,' she chuckled to Lisa, 'and that one him!'

'Too damned right,' Rorke agreed easily, apparently not in the slightest put out by her comment. He came round to Lisa's side of the bed and leaned over her, kissing her lightly on the mouth.

'Take Robbie downstairs and give him some breakfast,' he murmured, without lifting his eyes from her dazed face. 'And don't bring him back for at least an hour.'

Lisa's face was still hot when Mama Case closed the door behind her.

'How could you say that?' she accused bitterly. 'You know what she's going to think!'

'That I want to make long, leisurely love to you,' Rorke agreed calmly, 'and why not? She'll tell my father that we threw Robbie out so that we could be alone. He'll think everything's wonderful and start planning for the arrival of his grand-daughter, and I can start making plans for his operation . . .'

'And what if there isn't a granddaughter?' Lisa pressed bitterly, too furious to take him up on any of the other points. 'What if . . .'

'If that's a roundabout way of saying you want me to make love to you, all you have to do is go right ahead and say it,' Rorke murmured softly, never taking his eyes from her lips. 'I don't know how or where you've learned to make a man feel the way you do, Lisa—and part of me hates you because you can—but there's no denying that I want you, even knowing how many others have wanted you—and possessed you—before me.'

'Thanks a bunch!' she spat out bitterly. 'I suppose I'm expected to be thrilled by that admission. Well, I'm not, Rorke,' she told him bitterly, 'and as for providing Leigh with a granddaughter . . .'

'You're not going to co-operate? Never mind.' Rorke was actually laughing at her. 'Perhaps the damage is already done. I certainly wasn't holding anything back last night, and neither were you—were you, Lisa?'

Another minute and he would be forcing her to admit again how much she still wanted him. Already she could feel her breasts swelling, but fortunately the bedclothes concealed their betrayal from Rorke.

'You're a very sensual lover,' she told him. 'Naturally I . . .'

'Responded to me? Is that what you're going to say?' His mouth curled in a bitter sneer. 'But then any water is nectar to a thirsty man, isn't it, Lisa?

And it must be hard for you to have to snatch the odd embrace here and there while keeping your needs a secret from Robbie. 'What's that?' he demanded, as he caught her muttered, 'Go to hell!'

'One thing's for sure,' he drawled as he leaned over her, murmuring the words against her lips. 'If I do, I'm going to take you with me, and we both know how I can do that, don't we? Oh no, Lisa,' he murmured softly as she flinched away from him, 'I'm not playing games this time. Last night served its purpose, but there won't be a repetition—at least, I'm not going to initiate one.'

He got up and walked away from her, pausing by the bathroom door, to toss over his shoulder coolly,

'By the way, this room—we're sharing it, Lisa. Understand?'

She had to wait until he had gone before she could give in to the luxury of tears, shed alone in the privacy of the bathroom and haunted by the memory of how he had kissed away the ones she had cried the previous night. But last night was something she had to forget—if she was going to keep her sanity!

CHAPTER NINE

RORKE disappeared shortly after breakfast. He was flying to St Lucia, he told Lisa, but would be back after lunch.

Lisa took Robbie up to the hospital for his injections as she had promised Doctor James. Visiting the small island hospital reminded her of Mike Peters, and Rorke. She glanced down at Robbie's tousled head as Doctor James talked reassuringly to him, but Robbie wasn't afraid. He was very much his father in that respect, Lisa thought wryly, noticing how Robbie ignored the comforting hand she held out for him.

He hadn't forgiven her for allowing him to be banished from the bedroom this morning. She sighed. Her life seemed so fraught with problems she couldn't envisage ever being solved.

'Just a wee drop of blood now,' Doctor James, was saying comfortably to a white-faced but determined Robbie. 'Just to make sure there's plenty there.

'Do you know what blood group he is?' he asked Lisa. 'You'll know that his father's is extremely rare.'

'Robbie's too,' Lisa admitted. She had always worried a little that Robbie should inherit Rorke's rare blood group. She had only found out just after he was born, and she wondered what Rorke would say if she confronted him with it. She wasn't likely to find out, she decided grimly. She

was tired of trying to persuade Rorke to accept the
truth—she no longer cared what he believed; if
denying meant so much to his male pride then let
him. It wasn't the truth, but it went some way to
bolstering her pride—something which had
suffered considerably over the last few days. The
truth was that, weakly, she didn't want to hurt
him—which was ridiculous when she remembered
how much he had hurt her.

An old-fashioned boiled sweet did much to
restore Robbie to his normal good spirits, and
then they were free to leave.

Lisa drove back carefully. The island roads
could be treacherous in places. They were narrow
and winding, and she had always hated driving
along them.

Rorke returned just as she was about to take
Robbie upstairs for his nap.

Her mouth went dry and she longed to run
away. Coward, she mocked herself. What was she
afraid of? That Rorke would throw last night's
victory over her in her face?

'Lisa . . .' He walked towards her, lean and
bronzed, and her stomach muscles quivered in
agonised response. Why was she so weak?

'Lisa, I want to talk to you.'

'Not now, Rorke. I promised to go and see your
father. He has to rest in the afternoon and he gets
bored.'

A little to her surprise, Rorke didn't argue. In
fact Lisa noticed that he seemed almost tense.
What could he want to speak to her about?

'Tonight, then?' he suggested briefly. 'After
dinner?'

'In our room,' Lisa suggested.

'No! No,' Rorke said less sharply. 'We'll talk in
the library. We can be quite private in there.'

No more private than they could be in their
room, Lisa reflected. Why had he sounded so
angry when she suggested they talk there? She
shrugged aside the thought. If she started worrying
about whatever it was he wanted to talk to her
about now, she'd be a nervous wreck by tonight.

Leigh as always was pleased to see her. He looked
a little better today, she decided, watching him
carefully.

'Robbie tells me you took him to see Doctor
James this morning,' he smiled, as Lisa closed the
door of his pleasant sitting room.

She laughed. 'Yes. He needed to have some
injections. We left England in such a hurry that
there wasn't time for all of them.'

'He's a fine boy, Lisa.' He looked tired all of a
sudden. 'I can't tell you what it means to me to have
you both back here—to have you reunited with
Rorke. I should never have agreed to let him marry
you when you were so young. I told him as much at
the time, but I think, like me, he was frightened if he
didn't we'd lose you. Have you forgiven me?'

'There's nothing to forgive,' Lisa assured him,
kissing the papery skin of his cheek. 'I wanted to
marry Rorke—very, very much.

'And now,' she added, taking advantage of the
situation, 'I want you to get well enough to have
your operation—not just for our sakes, Leigh, but
for Robbie's as well. He needs you. I can vividly
remember how I longed to have a larger family,
and I very much want Robbie to have the chance
to get to know and love you.'

She could tell her words affected him. For a moment he said nothing, and then, shakily, 'I'll do my best—I'm not promising anything, mind, Lisa . . . but I'll certainly do my best.'

'That's all we ask.'

Ten minutes later she left him, having persuaded him to rest. If he could just get well enough to have his operation . . . She sighed, wondering if Robbie was awake. When they first arrived he had protested that sleeping in the afternoon was for babies, but now he went quite willingly to rest. After all, he was still adjusting to the heat, Lisa reflected, as she pushed open his bedroom door, her heart somersaulting as she looked for the tousled dark head and saw only the empty, rumpled bed. Mama Case walked into the room behind her, grinning when she saw Lisa.

'Mama, where's Robbie?'

'His daddy done take him down to the beach for a while, Miss Lisa,' Mama Case explained. 'Miss Helen, she came wanting Master Rorke to take her scuba-diving.' Mama Case's smile turned to a frown. 'She can't take no for an answer, that one.'

So Rorke had gone scuba-diving with Helen and they had taken Robbie with them! They were bound to have gone down to the cove, Lisa decided, stilling the maternal fears leaping to life inside her. It would do no harm to go down and keep an eye on things. Robbie loved the water, fortunately, and she knew Rorke well enough to be sure that he would take good care of the little boy. Even so . . .

It only took her fifteen minutes to walk down to the beach. She could see Rorke's discarded jeans and Robbie's shorts and shoes, and she shaded her

eyes, looking out to sea. The cove was protected
by a coral reef all round the bay; the water inside
it as calm and unruffled as the surface of a pond,
the surf moving softly against the silver sand.

On the sea side of the reef the surf pounded
unceasingly, throwing up spray and spume, and
Lisa wondered how far out Rorke had taken
Robbie. She remembered that when she was
barely a couple of years older than Robbie,
Rorke had taken her right out to the reef and
how thrilled she had been when he taught her
how to scuba. The underwater world was one
that had always fascinated her. Narrowing her
eyes against the sun, she searched the sea again,
frowning as she thought she glimpsed movement
over by the reef. Surely Rorke hadn't taken
Robbie out as far as that? Fear began to pound
inside her. Robbie was too young to go out so
far; such a very little boy.

Chiding herself, she tried to calm down. Were
all mothers like this with their children? Was she
becoming too possessive, too cautious, perhaps
smothering all Robbie's natural love of adventure?

As she watched she suddenly saw Helen emerge
from the sea and stand on the coral reef that jutted
dangerously out of the water. Coral was razor-
sharp, and cuts could be dangerous because they
became easily infected. Lisa vividly remembered
the lecture Rorke had once given her as a child
when she had fooled about on the coral. The
horrendous mental pictures he had drawn for her
of the consequences of her 'showing off' had
lingered in her mind for a long, long time.

Helen obviously thought she knew better, but
Lisa's heart was in her mouth when she saw

Robbie suddenly scramble up beside her. She longed to call to the little boy to warn him that what he was doing was dangerous, but she knew her voice wouldn't reach him. Where was Rorke? Why wasn't he watching him? In a fever of impatience, Lisa willed Rorke to appear, and then, before her horrified eyes, Robbie seemed to slip. Quite how it happened Lisa didn't know. One moment Helen was reaching down to help him up, the next the little boy was toppling back into the sea. In an agony of fear Lisa watched the water. Where was Rorke? She saw the sea, previously blue, suddenly turn an ominous dark red, and acting purely on instinct she ran into the water, swimming frantically to where she had last seen Robbie.

She had barely gone half a dozen lengths when she saw that Rorke was swimming strongly towards her, only he was swimming on his back, his body supporting Robbie's, and as they swam the red stain followed them.

Lisa reached the beach only seconds before Rorke. He didn't waste time speaking to her, simply pushing her aside as he laid Robbie on the sand and reached for his shirt.

'He cut himself on the coral. I think he got a vein.' All the time he was talking he was fashioning a tourniquet out of his shirt and a piece of stick he had picked up from the beach, working so quickly that Lisa's dazed mind could scarcely take it all in. Robbie looked so still and pale, lashes fluttering over the paper-white cheeks. Helen emerged from the sea, looking more bored than worried.

'God, Rorke,' she explained pettishly, 'why all

the fuss? I told you we should have left the kid behind.'

'Leave it, Helen,' Rorke advised without bothering to look at her, saying instead to Lisa, 'Run up to the house, will you, Lisa, and warn Dr James we're on our way. I'm not sure, but he may need a transfusion. Either way the cut will certainly have to be looked at.'

At that moment Robbie's lashes fluttered open. He stared first at Lisa, and she made a small, incoherent moan, longing to take him in her arms, but knowing that Rorke was far better equipped physically to carry him than she was, and she was already on her feet when Robbie turned to Helen and said quite clearly and very accusingly, 'You pushed me! You pushed me and I cut myself.'

Lisa didn't wait to hear what response Helen made to his accusation, she was far too anxious about Robbie's safety. In her own heart she was sure that Robbie was right and that Helen had pushed him, but she was equally sure that Helen would deny it and that Rorke would back her up. Why on earth had they taken Robbie with them, when all too obviously they had wanted to be alone?

By the time Lisa had phoned the hospital Rorke had arrived at the house. Lisa was on her way downstairs with a blanket to wrap Robbie in when she heard them arrive.

In no time at all they were in the Range Rover, Lisa sitting in the back with Robbie lying on the seat. His body felt cold and slight in her arms, and as Rorke eased the tourniquet slightly, sickness washed over her. This frail, quiet child was Robbie; her son, the child she had given birth to. Did all parents feel this helpless anguish when their child was seriously ill? She supposed they must, she thought vaguely, wondering a little at the numbing mist that seemed to have enveloped her. She knew that Robbie had cut himself badly, that he had lost a great deal of blood, and all that that implied, but she couldn't seem to think beyond getting him to the hospital; about fussing over small trifles that were really unimportant, as though by filling her mind with these trivia she could keep her real fear at bay.

Neither of them talked during the drive, although once when Rorke glanced in the driving mirror at her and saw the silent, anguished tears pouring down her face, he muttered, 'His father would have been flattered to see how much his child means to you. Would my child have meant as much, I wonder, Lisa?'

She couldn't even be bothered to respond. Robbie *was* his child, but she was tired of stating that fact and not being believed. All she wanted now was for Robbie to be safely installed at the hospital under Dr James's care.

Alerted to their arrival, nurses were ready to take Robbie from her as they pulled up outside. Pain tugged at her heart as she saw his tiny little frame being wheeled away.

'Try not to worry.'

She refused to look at Rorke. It was all right for him to say that. As far as he was concerned Robbie wasn't his child, and he couldn't really care less what harm his girl-friend might have done to him.

'There's a waiting area round here, let's go and sit down,' he suggested. 'I'll get us both a cup of coffee.'

'Don't bother, I'm perfectly happy to wait on my own. You might as well go back to Helen—I don't want to spoil your afternoon together.'

She had her back to Rorke and just caught the explosive mutter of fury, before he swung her round, his eyes bleak and grim.

'Look, it may suit you to cast me as the cold, unfeeling villain of the piece, but it so happens that I do care about Robbie, and I am going to stay here.'

'You should never have taken him out there!'

There, she had said it, and had the satisfaction of seeing Rorke pale beneath his tan.

'Lisa, I . . .' he began, but Dr James was coming towards them, and Lisa no longer cared what excuses Rorke was about to make, her whole attention was concentrated on the doctor.

'Robbie—is he . . .'

'He's fine,' he interrupted her gently. 'Or at least he will be once we give him a transfusion. He's lost quite a lot of blood—it's lucky that you weren't away when this happened, Rorke,' he was saying to the other man, while Lisa's face tightened in bitterness. If Rorke had been away the accident wouldn't have happened in the first place. 'If you'll just go with Nurse, she'll do the necessary and . . .'

Rorke was frowning, and Lisa's heart skipped a beat as she heard him say curtly, 'I don't think I understand—are you suggesting that . . .'

'Dr James knows that you and Robbie share the same blood group, Rorke,' Lisa interrupted quickly, too concerned for Robbie now to spare Rorke's feelings. What on earth was Dr James going to think if Rorke started denying that

Robbie was his son, when he had irrefutable evidence that he was?

'That's right,' Dr James agreed with a smile. 'In fact I was only remarking on it this morning to Lisa. Of course it's by no means unusual for a child to inherit a blood group from its father, but yours is such a rare one that it's fortunate for Robbie that you're here—I noticed this morning that we don't have any in reserve. When Mike Peters was here he started up a blood bank, and got most of the islanders to give blood—by first donating a pint of his own, I remember him telling me. Like most doctors he doesn't particularly like sticking needles in himself, and as he told me at the time, giving a pint of his own blood was purely symbolic, as he belongs to a very common blood group. However, it seemed to do the trick, but I seem to remember that you needed a transfusion a couple of years ago when you had that accident down by the harbour, and we never got you in to give any more.'

Lisa could tell by Rorke's rigidly stiff back that Dr James's revelation had come as a shock. In other circumstances she might almost have been able to feel pity for the grimly haunted face he turned towards her when Dr James had finished speaking, but now all she could think of was Robbie. Robbie injured and in need of the life-giving blood that had to come from his father.

'Rorke.'

Dr James was touching him lightly on the shoulder, indicating the waiting nurse. Lisa couldn't bear to watch as Rorke followed her down the corridor, and she wasn't even aware that Dr James had remained until he said gently, 'Try not to worry. I promise you he's going to be all right. It's lucky for him that you brought him in for those boosters so quickly, Lisa, and that Rorke was on hand. What happened exactly?'

Now was her chance to implicate Helen by repeating what Robbie had said to her, but she found she just wasn't able to do so. All her attention was concentrated on Robbie, willing him to get well. She simply told Dr James that Robbie had slipped on the coral and gashed his arm.

'Yes, I thought that's what must have happened. Robbie told me that Rorke hadn't wanted to take him on to the reef, but that he had insisted on going. He's a very lucky little boy,' he added a trifle grimly. 'Thank God Rorke kept a cool enough head to act quickly, otherwise . . .'

'Please . . . when can I see Robbie?' Lisa asked him urgently. Her throat muscles were taut with tension, she felt oddly lightheaded and yet strangely weak, almost as though she could float away. As she followed Dr James down the corridor she had the oddest sense of weightlessness, almost of not really being there at all, but separate from her body, watching its mechanical movements.

The ward Robbie was in was a small one; the other beds were empty apart from the one next to him where Rorke lay, watching the little boy, his arm brown and sinewy against the white of the bedclothes and the complication of the transfusion equipment.

Even as she watched Lisa could see a more natural colour returning to Robbie's pale face. She had eyes only for her son, unaware of the pain etched into Rorke's features as he watched.

Dr James's light touch on her shoulder roused her. 'Look,' he said quietly, 'Robbie's starting to come round. We gave him a tranquillising shot when you brought him in. He's a tough little character,' he added for Rorke's benefit, 'and something tells me this isn't the last time I'm going to see him here.'

'In that case I'd better come in again and give you some more of this,' Rorke told him, tapping the tube linking his arm to the transfusion equipment. 'Another time I might not be on hand.'

'Good idea,' Dr James agreed, indicating to the nurse that Rorke could get up.

Robbie stirred and opened his eyes, and to Lisa's anguish the first person he looked for was Rorke.

'I'm sorry I went on the reef when you told me not to, Daddy,' he said drowsily.

'That's all right, Robbie.' Rorke swung himself off the bed and crouched down beside the little boy. 'You've learned a painful lesson, and you know now why I was warning you not to climb on the coral.'

'But Helen did it,' Robbie objected sleepily.

'Helen's old enough to make her own mistakes,' Lisa heard Rorke saying huskily. He saw Dr James glancing at him and added softly, 'Now you're going to go to sleep for a little while.'

'Will you be here when I wake up?'

Across the bed Rorke's eyes met Lisa's.

'We'll both be here Robbie,' he promised softly.

With a little sigh Robbie turned to Lisa, letting her kiss and cuddle him, telling her drowsily that he was all right.

They left the ward together, Lisa unable to

forget that Robbie had turned first to his father. She was still in a numb daze when she stumbled against the wall. Instantly Rorke's arm was supporting her and it seemed from the dream world she was suddenly inhabiting that there was pain as well as concern in the look he gave her. From a distance she heard Dr James's voice answering Rorke's sharply curt query, and then she was sliding into warm darkness, the voices of the two men dull echoes that couldn't hurt or touch her.

'Lisa!'

She recognised the voice and its implicit command and opened her eyes warily. She was lying in the bed she shared with Rorke, although she had no memory of getting there. Rorke himself was standing beside the bed, staring down at her, his face tautly bitter. Lisa's hand crept up to the pulse beating erratically in her throat, encountering the soft silk of her nightgown. Who had undressed her and put her to bed? Rorke? Heated colour flooded her skin as she caught the elusive memory of gentle hands easing her out of her clothes, soothing her anguished protests.

'Lisa, I know you're awake. I want to talk to you.'

'I know,' she agreed huskily, 'you've already told me.'

She looked up and saw that Rorke was frowning. 'That was before . . .'

'Before you found out that Robbie is your son?'

Strange how knowing that he now knew the truth had so little effect upon her. She ought to be exulting, but somehow it was too much of an effort. All she cared about was Robbie. Rorke had denied his child for too long for her to care that he knew the truth now. Where once she would have given anything to have him standing looking at her with the helpless anguish she could read plainly in his eyes, suddenly it meant less than nothing to her. It was almost as though she were incapable of feeling anything. It was a sensation not unlike the numbing anaesthetic administered by her dentist. She knew what was happening around her, she knew how she ought to react to it, but somehow the numbing effect of the anaethestic made it impossible for her to do anything more than be an onlooker.

'Lisa, for God's sake! I didn't know . . . . I couldn't believe . . .'

She turned away from him, her voice cool as she said quietly, 'It really doesn't matter any more, Rorke. Loving someone sometimes does require an act of faith. It isn't your fault that you couldn't believe me—not when you couldn't remember what happened.'

'Dr James says you're suffering from shock and that you must rest, but we have to talk this whole thing out, Lisa, we can't just leave it here.'

'Why not?' She was amazed that she could be so calm, so uncaring in what ought to have been her moment of triumph.

She heard Rorke growl something in his throat, but didn't bother to turn round.

'You might have just discovered that Robbie is your son, Rorke, but don't forget I've always known, and so for me nothing has changed.'

'We'll talk about it later,' she heard Rorke say grimly as he got up and left the room, closing the door quietly behind him. Once he had gone she gave herself up to the desire to sleep, wondering vaguely if Dr James had given her some sort of tranquillising shot. She felt so calm and relaxed.

It was some time later that she heard her bedroom door open again. This time it wasn't Rorke, it was Helen, immaculately dressed in a suit of pure gentian blue silk, her eyes hardening as they looked across the distance that separated them.

'You haven't won, you know,' she began conversationally, sitting down and crossing slender brown legs. 'You might think that discovering that Robbie is really his son is going to make Rorke turn to you, but it won't, Lisa. In fact,' she continued, idly smoothing the silk fabric with long, painted nails, an expression of feline triumph in her eyes, 'it simply makes matters easier for us.'

'If you mean by "easier" that Rorke can divorce me to marry you, he's been free to do that for the last five years,' Lisa told her calmly.

'Oh yes, but then he's always known how much his father dotes on you. Leigh had planned to split his estate between the two of you, you know, until he found out about the boy. Now he's leaving your share to Robbie, and as Rorke is Robbie's natural father, it will be the easiest thing in the world for him to divorce you and claim custody. That way he keeps Leigh happy by keeping the child here and he gets to inherit the entire estate.' She laughed softly. 'Now that Rorke knows that Robbie is his son he holds the winning card doesn't he?'

Half an hour later when Mama Case came upstairs with a glass of milk and some fruit she found Lisa staring blindly out of the window, her face pale and set.

'Why, honey chile, whatever be de matter?' she exclaimed in concern. 'That little boy, him gonna be just fine, so don't you go worryin' yourself about him.'

So Robbie was going to be 'just fine', was he? A huge lump gathered in Lisa's throat. What would Mama Case say if she told her how callously Rorke was planning to take her son from her? If only she could appeal to Leigh for help—but how could she in his present weakened state? What on earth was she going to do? Panic tore into her. She wanted to go and see Robbie to make sure that he was all right, that Helen and Rorke hadn't spirited him away somewhere. One read about such horrible things she thought feverishly, of parents snatching their children or all manner of dreadful things. Tears started to stream down her face, and she saw Mama Case watching her with growing concern. She went to the door and opened it, calling something. Ten minutes later Rorke came into the room, his face grim and unreadable. Did he know that Helen had told her the truth? She suspected not. Rorke was too skilled a tactician to want her to be forewarned of what he planned.

'Lisa, stop tearing yourself apart,' he commanded sternly, 'Robbie is going to be all right. If you want the truth Dr James is more concerned about you. He seems to think you're going through some sort of crisis brought on by the strain of Robbie's accident. Drink this milk and take this tablet. It's only to help you sleep,' he added sardonically, seeing her expression. 'I'm not Bluebeard. I'm not about to do away with you.'

Under his grim gaze she was forced to take the
pill and swallow it down with milk, and although
she fought hard against the darkness reaching out
to engulf her, it proved too strong. She found
herself sinking into it, Rorke's face growing misty
and distant, the smile he gave her as she finally
went under terrifying in its triumph. Her last
thought was that somehow she must get Robbie
away. She must prevent Rorke from doing what
Helen said he planned to do. Helen already had
her husband, she thought bitterly, she wasn't going
to have her son as well.

A terrible presentiment of evil stalked her through
her dreams; the old childhood nightmare of being
pursued through some tangled leafless forest of
gaunt spectral trees by some terrifying but unseen
'thing', resurrected as she tried desperately to
escape the fear haunting her.

A sudden sharp sound splintered through her
fear and she woke up staring round the darkened
room, her mouth dry and her heart pounding with
fear.

'It's all right, Lisa.' Rorke's voice reached her
through the darkness and she realised the sound
that woke her must have been him entering the
room.

'You've been having a bad dream so Mama
Case says. She didn't know whether to wake you
or not. Would you like a drink?'

'Fruit juice please.' She felt so dry. It must be
the tablet he had given her. 'Rorke, Robbie . . .'

'He's fine,' he assured her briefly. 'We should be
able to bring him home in a couple of days.'

The words 'we' and 'home' started off an ache inside her that wouldn't be stilled. She moved restlessly in the large bed, wishing she had the courage to ask Rorke to leave. Where before she had felt protected from any kind of pain, now her reactions were just the opposite. Her emotions felt raw and bruised, tears far too near the surface, her body crying out for the comfort of Rorke's arms, the solace of his lovemaking, and yet she knew quite well that neither could ease the real pain because that sprang from the knowledge that he didn't want her, didn't love her, and planned to deprive her of her child.

'Here's your juice.'

He had moved so quickly and quietly she hadn't seen him. As she reached up to take the glass her fingers were trembling so much that some of the liquid splashed over her skin.

Instantly Rorke was bending over her, his arm supporting her as he sat on the bed lifting her and holding the glass for her so that she could drink in comfort.

'Lisa, we have to talk.'

She stiffened immediately.

'What about?' she asked coldly. 'We don't have anything to speak about, Rorke.'

'We have Robbie,' he contradicted quietly. 'He's my son, Lisa.'

'He's been your son from the moment he was conceived, but somehow that fact hasn't bothered you before!'

She felt him tense, and in the moonlight saw the dull colour edging up under his skin.

He was about to say something when the door opened and Mama Case came bustling in.

'You all right?' she asked Lisa. 'Tossing and turning like nobody's business you were.'

'I was having a bad dream,' she admitted. 'But I'm fine now.'

'You always did feel fine when Master Rorke was around,' Mama Case chuckled. 'Even as a little girl. Every time you fell over, he always had to be the one to kiss you better.'

She was still laughing as she left the room, but Lisa felt as though her heart was being squeezed in a vice. Rorke was watching her intently, and to her dismay he lifted his hand, tracing the outline of her jaw and smoothing the untidy curls back off her hot face.

'You put me on a pedestal, Lisa,' he said huskily, 'and now you can't forgive me for falling off it, but I could still try to kiss you better.'

Lisa wouldn't allow herself to believe that that was a plea she could hear beneath the quiet words.

'It's too late, Rorke,' she told him icily. 'Five years too late.'

She had turned her back, but she heard him get up and move around the room, and there was a tight bitterness in his voice as he said slowly, 'I suppose I ought to have expected that, but somehow I hoped you wouldn't say it. I'll get Mama Case to come up and sit with you. Goodnight, Lisa.'

When he had gone she wanted to cry, but couldn't. She had cried too much already. Somehow she had to find a way to leave St Martins with Robbie, and quickly. If she could just get to St Lucia. But how? And then it came to her. She could telephone over to St Lucia and get them to send a plane for her. She could tell them that Rorke wanted it. There was a kind of bitter satisfaction to be found in letting him pay for their escape. Tomorrow she was going to the hospital to see Robbie and to find out from Dr James how long it would be before the little boy could leave, and nobody, but nobody was going to stop her.

CHAPTER TEN

Lisa was dismayed to realise how shaky she felt. Mama Case had shaken her head when she told her she was going to the hospital, but nothing she could do could dissuade her.

Rorke had been away, down at the harbour supervising some work on *Lady*, so Lisa got one of the boys to drive her to the hospital.

Robbie was cheerfully happy to see her, and kept asking about Rorke. How was he going to react when he learned that he wasn't likely to see his father again? Would he hate her for it? After all, he was Rorke's son, and seemed to have inherited from him Rorke's love of St Martin's. But she couldn't allow Rorke to take him away from her. She just didn't have that kind of strength.

Dr. James explained to her that they wanted to keep Robbie in for a few days, but told her that she could come and see him as often as she wanted. 'But what about you, lassie?' he asked gently. 'You're tearing yourself apart and it isn't doing you any good.'

'I'll be all right,' she assured him, brushing aside his concern. The only thing that could ever make her 'all right' again was Rorke's love, and she was as likely to get that as she was to fly to the moon.

She was just leaving the hospital when she saw Rorke crossing the road towards her. She turned blindly away, not wanting to confront him again before she was able to get herself under control. The sun was shining in her eyes and she was vaguely aware of the sound of a car horn, and then everything blurred into a mist as something seemed to hit her in the solar plexus and she collapsed, gasping for breath.

When she came round she was back in the hospital with Dr James smiling wryly down at her.

'Lassie, lassie, what were you thinking of? he chided. 'Have you forgotten what side of the road we drive on over here?'

She had done, Lisa realised guiltily, and she had darted across the road in her anxiety to escape Rorke, without looking properly.

'I did,' she admitted shakily. 'Did something hit me?'

'Not "something" but someone,' Dr James told her grimly, 'Fortunately Rorke has quick reflexes. He managed to get to you before the car did, and took the brunt of the impact. You were winded when he pushed you out of the way. He saved your life, Lisa,' he told her quietly, with a look in his eyes that told her he saw more than she had thought.

'I . . . is he all right?' she asked shakily,

'Apart from a nasty bruise on his thigh and a knock on the head he's fine. But I want to keep him in for a few days—just in case there's any delayed concussion. Funny thing, concussion.'

'Yes, so I believe,' Lisa agreed, smiling bitterly. She already knew the potentially disastrous effects of concussion. How feverishly she had read up on the effects of it in the months leading up to Robbie's birth.

Dr James told her she could go and see Rorke,

but added that he was under sedation and so Lisa refused, offering as an excuse the fact that she wanted to get back and reassure Leigh that everything was all right before he heard a garbled and embroidered version of what had happened via the island grapevine.

She found him in his study, and although he paled a little when she told him what had happened he was quickly reassured.

She knew she ought to tell Leigh what she was planning, but she simply couldn't bring herself to do so. Perhaps if she were to write him a letter explaining? She had no wish to cause him any pain—far from it, but she was determined that she wasn't going to lose Robbie. As she left her eye was caught by half a dozen familiar dust jackets on the shelves with the other books—her own illustrations! How had they come to be there? Following her glance Leigh turned—'Rorke bought them,' he told her quietly. 'They were all he had of you.'

'You not putting on a pretty dress to visit Rorke?' Mama Case questioned disapprovingly as she watched Lisa comb her hair and add a coating of soft pink gloss to her lips.

'I doubt if he'll care what I'm wearing,' Lisa told her wryly, checking her appearance in the full-length mirror, while Mama Case shook her head disapprovingly.

This time Lisa drove to the hospital alone. Dr James assured her that Robbie was doing fine. 'He'll be able to come home in a day or two—if just to give my nurses a rest, although Rorke has been with him this morning. He's been asking when you were coming.' Dr James didn't add anything, but Lisa could tell that he was a little surprised that she hadn't mentioned Rorke or asked after him. She had been too busy feverishly working out when to order the plane for. No one apart from herself need know. She could telephone from the house and then make some excuse to get Robbie and herself out of the house at the requisite time. They would just have to leave their luggage behind—it was better to do that than risk someone guessing what she was doing.

Realising that Dr James was still watching her, Lisa said hurriedly, 'Oh yes, of course, I'll go and see him now. I wasn't sure if he was allowed visitors yet.'

'He tends to have a mind of his own,' Dr James told her dryly, 'and he doesn't like being confined to bed. Although I must say I've found him a far more docile patient than I expected. He seems to have a great deal of interest in the subject of concussion and its after-effects. He told me that he hadn't realised that it could cause lapses of memory.'

Lisa refused to be drawn. She was sure Dr James suspected something, but she wasn't going to enlighten him.

'I'll just go and see Rorke. Where is he?'

'We've put him in a private room just down the corridor. First on your left.'

The door was open and as Lisa approached she could hear raised voices—Rorke's and Helen's. She hesitated, not wanting to intrude and yet wondering what they were discussing.

'You know my views on the subject,' she heard Rorke saying tersely. 'I've told you often enough before, Helen . . .'

Lisa didn't stay to hear Helen's reply. She wasn't sure what they were discussing, but suddenly it was more than her frail self-control could bear to stand there listening to her husband talking to his mistress. They sounded as though they were quarrelling, but she could vividly imagine how the quarrel would end—with Helen in Rorke's arms, and his mouth silencing her protests. She remembered Leigh telling her quietly that Rorke had bought the books she had illustrated—Why? To feed his resentment of her?

When she left the hospital Lisa didn't go straight back to the house. She needed time to think—to plan, and she parked the car on a lonely stretch of road, leaving it while she walked along the sand, listening to the breeze stirring the palms. She must have walked miles, she realised later as she climbed back into the car. Her thigh muscles were aching and she felt very tired. It was growing dark too—she tended to forget how swiftly dusk fell out here, and she paused before starting the engine, watching the crimson and orange glory of the dying sun, acknowledging that there would be few opportunities to do so again.

She loved St Martins, she loved the peace and solitude; London had never really held any allure for her, it was simply a place where she could work and earn enough money to keep herself and Robbie. Robbie! Her heart thudded guiltily. Did she have the right to take him away from all this? Of course she did, she assured herself firmly, squashing all her doubts. She was his mother!

It was dark when she drove up to the house. She knew that Leigh had gone to visit his friend across the other side of the island and that they would be

playing chess together. It was also the evening that
Mama Case visited her family in the village. Lisa
knew she ought to go and have something to eat—
she had barely touched her lunch, but she had no
appetite. Instead she decided to go upstairs and
have a bath. She could read in bed for a couple of
hours, it might help her unwind. Her nerves felt
like over-wound springs, her shoulder muscles
tense and sensitive to every movement around her.

As she opened the bedroom door she sensed
that all was not as it should be, but she was inside
before she realised what was wrong—inside and
confronting her was a furiously angry Rorke who
was sitting up in their bed, his face contorted into
a mask of rage.

'Where the hell have you been?' he breathed
softly. His body was bare to the waist, and in spite
of her resolution Lisa was powerless to stop the
frisson of awareness coursing through her as she
looked at the smooth tanned skin, roughened by
the dark body hair covering his chest and arrowing
down past his navel.

'Rorke! What are you doing here?' The words
jerked out past grimly compressed lips, and she
could tell from the look in his eyes that Rorke had
caught the note of hysterical despair underlying
them.

'Dr James said I could come home.' As he spoke
he was flinging back the bedclothes, apparently
oblivious to the fact that he was completely naked,
and Lisa averted her eyes hurriedly, looking round
for his robe and saying huskily, 'Rorke, I don't
think you should be out of bed.'

'Then don't make it so damned difficult for me
to talk to you! Ever since I learned the truth

you've been so bloody elusive. Why, Lisa? I should have thought you'd have enjoyed the opportunity to gloat, to fling it all back in my face—well, here's something else you can gloat about,' he told her savagely. 'When I was hit by that car, everything came back to me—don't ask me to explain how or why, it just did; a small series of haunting but very real pictures. I remembered everything,' he said flatly, breathing heavily, 'Every damn thing.'

There was no way she could avoid looking at him. He seemed to will her into doing so, and her breath caught as she saw the anguish in the over-bright eyes, the pain that the locked muscles and tensed jaw couldn't quite control. All at once, for no good reason at all she was overwhelmed by compassion and love. She ought to be gloating, she recognised; she ought at the very least to use this moment of weakness to force Rorke to give up all claim to Robbie, but somehow she found herself saying gently, as though he were in fact Robbie in pain and needing her comfort, 'Rorke, it's not your fault. Mike explained it to me at the time.' She went towards him, terrified when she saw him sway slightly, her arms going out to support him as she urged him back towards the bed. Only somehow he wasn't moving. In fact his arms were going round her, his mouth, hot and shaking slightly, burning into her skin as he buried his face in the curve of her shoulder.

'I remember this, Lisa,' he muttered thickly, pushing aside the neck of her tee-shirt and caressing the skin he had bared with undisguised passion, 'and this . . .' His hands were under her tee-shirt, cupping the burgeoning fullness of her breasts, his groan of mingled anguish and need melting the barriers she had raised against him.

Somehow they were both on the bed, Rorke trembling and shivering as he pulled her against him, tugging impatiently at her tee-shirt, releasing the zip on her jeans, huskily muttering his need as he wrenched aside her tee-shirt and unclipped her bra, his touch burning into her skin as he caressed her exposed breasts with a hunger that seemed to take her backwards in time.

His body seemed to burn to her touch as though he had a fever, his eyes brilliant and over-bright in the darkness, closing briefly as she touched him, tentatively as first and then more surely as he murmured his pleasure and need before burying his hot face between her breasts, then caressing them with his lips until she was aroused as he was himself; touching his body as urgently as he touched hers, the night air full of their incoherent murmurs.

He raised his head and Lisa could feel him watching her through the darkness. Her heart pounded unsteadily, everything forgotten but the fact that this was the man she loved; and she did love him, with her heart and her mind as well as her body.

'I remember this,' Rorke whispered softly, touching his lips to one tautly aroused nipple, 'and this . . .' He caressed the other in the same fashion, his hands stroking down to her hips. 'I remember exactly how much I wanted you, and how sweetly you gave yourself to me. I hurt you, Lisa, and you cried, and I hated myself for breaking all the vows I'd made to myself and my father. You were seventeen . . .' He was breathing heavily, his eyes glittering in a face suddenly stripped of every defence. 'God, how I wanted you ... and God, how I hated myself afterwards! Perhaps I didn't want to remember, Lisa, but that gives me no excuse, and to accuse you of taking Peters as your lover ...' He moved restlessly. 'If you want the truth, I was always jealous of him. You seemed to enjoy his company; I'd seen the two of you together, found you together in his bungalow ...'

'He knew I wasn't well,' Lisa told him. 'He suspected I might be pregnant. He was just checking. He warned me to tell you, Rorke. I had to tell him about what had happened—how you couldn't remember. He warned me to tell you, but the opportunity never came ...'

'And I rejected you when you did try to tell me. I couldn't let myself believe it, but I paid a heavy price for my pride, Lisa!

His voice was filled with self-hatred, and once again Lisa felt compassion fill her. What was it about loving someone that made you able to accept all their faults? Perhaps he was right, perhaps then she had put him on a pedestal. Now she loved him as an equal, but he didn't love her, no matter how much he might desire her.

'Lisa!' She heard him sigh against her skin. 'I can't even ask you to forgive me, to do so would be an outrageous arrogance, how could anyone forgive such a crime?' Lisa felt him tremble against her and was overwhelmed by a longing to comfort him. She took him in her arms, instinctively holding him as though he were Robbie, trying to find the words, to take the pain out of his eyes. His skin seemed to burn against her, and she realised that he wasn't Robbie and that she wanted him—badly. She felt him move restlessly in her embrace, his voice thick and husky as he muttered, 'Lisa, for God's sake, I'm not made of stone . . .'

Neither was she, and when she left she wanted to take with her the memory of this night together; the pleasure of being in his arms, of being part of him, and so instead of releasing him, she let her lips wander over the smooth skin of his shoulder, her fingers trailing provocatively along the length of his body. She felt his tense withdrawal almost immediately, wincing at the expletive he muttered jerkily, his eyes almost black in the moonlight as he realised she was deliberately tormenting him and that she wasn't going to stop. For one brief moment Lisa thought he was going to recover his self-control. She could almost feel his tension— and then with a smothered groan he slid his fingers into her hair, tilting her head back, his eyes hot, hectic colour burning up under his skin as he looked at her.

She wasn't seventeen any longer. She loved him and she wanted him, and suddenly it was easy to let the seductive curves of her body, silvered by the moonlight, whisper their own message to him. Her heart was thumping as he lowered his mouth to hers, and she could feel his own pounding heavily against her. He kissed her lightly, his mouth merely brushing hers, but Lisa could feel the hard arousal of his body against her, and laced her fingers behind his neck, letting her lips part invitingly beneath his, a fierce surge of pleasure lancing through her as she felt the sweat break out across his chest, his body trembling violently against hers as his control slid away and his mouth moved urgent and demanding over hers, depriving

her of breath, depriving her of everything but the
need to respond to, and match, the fierce tumult of
desire that possessed him.

Now it was too late to turn back, and she had
no desire to do so, Lisa admitted as her body
responded passionately to Rorke's touch. Now it
was her turn to protest as his hands stroked over
her skin, caressing and arousing, inciting her body
to arch wantonly beneath his, welcoming the hard
pressure of his thighs as they parted hers, her
fingers tensing into the hard muscles of his back as
his mouth closed over hers in a kiss that echoed his
fiercely hungry possession of her body.

It was only later, when the glow of satisfaction
had faded and the memory of what he intended to
do returned, that Lisa regretted what she had
done—not for herself, but for Robbie. For
Robbie's sake she ought to have been strong.

Rorke, strangely enough, seemed reluctant to
release her, keeping her within the circle of his
arms, his body still tangled with hers, as though he
couldn't bear to let her go. She tried to move away
and his grip tightened.

'Don't move,' he murmured throatily, his lips
brushing the exposed skin of her shoulder. 'I never
want you out of touching distance again, Lisa.'

'I should think Helen will have something to say
about that,' she reminded him bitterly. 'Oh, it's all
right, Rorke,' she added before he could speak, 'I
know the truth. I know you intend to divorce me
and fight to get custody of Robbie so that you can
inherit all your father's estate, but I'm not going to
let you do it. You can divorce me if you wish,
but . . .'

'Divorce you?' He raised himself up on one

elbow and stared down at her, his voice bitterly incredulous. 'Just what the hell are you talking about, Lisa? You know damn well I'd never divorce you. God, I wrote to you often enough telling you that, begging you to come back to me, Robbie or no Robbie. Five long years I've been without you, Lisa. Five long years when you've haunted me to the point of madness. I found your books in a shop on St Lucia, a woman was buying one and when she opened it I saw your name inside. I bought the lot. I even tried to discover your address from the publishers, but they weren't having any. I was like a man possessed, Lisa, wanting you, hating you, hating myself, convinced that you had lied. I've had a long talk with Dr James,' he said suddenly changing the subject, 'about my loss of memory. He ascribes it to guilt, and I suspect he's right. I couldn't remember because I didn't want to remember how I had broken my vow to myself, so instead I accused you.' His voice thickened unsteadily. 'God, when I think . . .'

'Then don't,' Lisa advised him softly, remembering how he had claimed in London that it would destroy him to believe that she had told the truth.

'I never stopped wanting you, Lisa,' he told her huskily, 'and when my father became ill and wanted to see you it gave me another chance to come and look for you. The ideal excuse to get you back here; back into my life, in my home, in my bed, and in my arms, Lisa, and now that you're here, there's no way I'm ever going to let you go. Why did you never even answer my letters? Did you hate me so much?'

'I never got them,' Lisa told him simply. 'I never even went to the bank where you opened an account for me. How did you find me, Rorke?' she questioned.

'I used a private detective. I showed him your books, told him your name, and he did the rest.'

'And you still wanted me, even though you . . .'

'Even though I thought you had another lover?' He pushed irate fingers through his hair. 'God, Lisa, you know by now how I feel about you, surely? Yes, I was as bitter and as hurt as hell when I thought you'd given yourself to someone else. For a time I think I went right out of my mind. But I loved you. I loved you and I couldn't let you go . . .'

'You loved me?' Her eyes were huge in her pale face.

'You doubt it? After tonight's performance?' he asked with dry incredulity. 'Lisa my love, you can't be that innocent. You must have learned something about men in the years we've been apart.'

'The only things I know about the male sex are those I've learned from you and Robbie,' Lisa told him wryly, too shaken by his admissions to pretend. A kind of fierce excitement was burning through her body, a tension that threatened to tear her in two, but she refused to give way to it. 'I thought you merely desired me. I was too young to talk properly to you, Rorke, and when Helen told me you merely desired me . . . She told me you wanted a divorce,' she added, recalling her most recent conversation with the other woman, and pain darkened her eyes momentarily.

'Helen's been pushing for that ever since you left

me, but she knows exactly where she stands,' Rorke remarked dryly, 'and it isn't next to me—not now, not ever.'

'It was partially because of her that I left,' Lisa admitted weakly. 'She told me you wanted me, but she said if it wasn't for Leigh and my position in the family, you'd have simply had an affair with me. She said you would get tired of me, and then there was Robbie . . .'

'If it hadn't been for Leigh I'd have smuggled you on board *Lady* and sailed off with you a long time before I did,' Rorke admitted. 'But I'd still have married you, Lisa, don't make any mistake about that. Any doubts I had concerned your feelings for me, not mine for you. You're forgetting I was an adult male, you were still a child, I couldn't help feeling guilty about trapping you into a relationship you weren't ready for. Oh, I knew I could arouse you . . .' he laughed when he saw her expression, 'and you'll never know how tempted I was to do so at times . . . but I wanted you to love me as an adult woman.'

'And now?' Lisa asked hesitantly.

'And now,' Rorke retorted lazily, smiling at her, 'you are a grown woman, and I still love you and want you very much.' His expression changed suddenly, becoming almost tortured. 'I can still arouse you, Lisa.' He glanced down at her body and his expression made her pulses leap. 'But I want more than that,' he told her huskily. 'I want your love too.'

She looked at him, wondering if she was actually hearing correctly. He had said he still loved her, but . . . She heard him give a muffled imprecation and then she was in his arms, his lips against her skin. 'Don't look at me like that,' he muttered hoarsely. 'God knows you've every reason to doubt and mistrust me . . .'

But had she? Would she have felt the same if she'd known that he had wanted her back, written to her? Couldn't she, now that she knew the full story, understand a little better? Didn't she, after all, still love him?

'I don't doubt you, Rorke,' she said softly, wondering at how true the words were once she had voiced them. 'I hated it when I thought you were going to divorce me and marry Helen. There's never been anyone but you,' she admitted shakily, 'and I still love you so much it makes me ache inside.'

'Helen knows exactly what I think of her—I've told her often enough, but she persists in clinging. I could have murdered her when she insisted on joining Robbie and me the other day, especially when she persuaded him to climb up on to that coral.'

'Do you think she really pushed him?' Lisa asked hesistantly.

'I don't know. I suspect there's a strong possibility, although I couldn't get her to admit it. What I have done, though, is suggested that in future, if she's wise, she'll think of a watertight excuse whenever her uncle invites her to stay with him. I don't want her on St Martins ever again. God, when I saw your face when you looked at Robbie! Of course I was concerned for the boy—almost against my will I found I liked him, but it tore me apart to see you destroying yourself over another man's child. However, that was nothing to the agony I faced when I discovered he was actually mine,' Rorke told her in a low tortured voice. His face had gone pale, and Lisa could almost feel the raw agony he was enduring.

'It's over now, Rorke,' she comforted him, 'and in some ways I can't be sorry. I'm glad you know the truth, although when it happened I felt too numb; too concerned about Robbie to care about anything else.'

'And now?' he murmured against her throat, and in spite of his caress and the casual tone of his question Lisa could feel the tension emanating from him, the tautness of his body as he waited for her response.

'And now,' she told him gently,' I find that there is something I care about as much as, if not more than, Robbie, and that's your love, Rorke. For years I've told myself I didn't care? I didn't love you any more; I hated you, but none of it was true. When I opened my front door and saw you standing there I knew how untrue it was. It was all I could do to stop myself flinging myself into your arms.'

'And it was all I could do not to take you into them,' Rorke admitted, adding in a voice that told her he was smiling. 'However, there's nothing to stop either of us giving in to our instincts now, is there?'

There wasn't, and Lisa went joyously into his arms, echoing the husky words of love he murmured against her skin, breathing in the warm, male scent of him as his fingers touched her body.

She was home, truly home at last, and she wondered that she could ever have hoped to find it anywhere but there, in Rorke's arms.

Harlequin® *Plus*

A WORD ABOUT THE AUTHOR

Born in Preston, a small city north of Liverpool, England, Penny Jordan was constantly in trouble as a schoolgirl because of her inability to stop daydreaming—the first sign of possible talent as a writer! When she was not daydreaming, she spent most of her spare time curled up somewhere with a book. Early in her teens, she was introduced to romance novels and became an avid reader, but at the time it didn't occur to her to try to write one herself.

That changed when she entered her thirties and felt an urge to make a mark in the world by means of her own talent. She had many false starts — lots of "great" ideas ended up in the wastepaper basket. But finally the day came when Penny completed her first book-length manuscript. And, to her utter amazement, it wasn't long before the novel was accepted for publication.

Now she has received many letters of acceptance for her books, and every letter brings the thrill of knowing that the stories on which she has worked so hard will reach the readers for whom each is lovingly written.

Share the joys and sorrows
of real-life love with
Harlequin American Romance!™

GET THIS BOOK
FREE as your introduction to
Harlequin American Romance—
an exciting series of romance
novels written especially for
the American woman of today.

Mail to:
Harlequin Reader Service

In the U.S.
2504 West Southern Avenue
Tempe, AZ 85282

In Canada
649 Ontario Street
Stratford, Ontario N5A 6W2

YES! I want to be one of the first to discover
Harlequin American Romance. Send me FREE and without
obligation *Twice in a Lifetime.* If you do not hear from me after I
have examined my FREE book, please send me the 4 new
Harlequin American Romances each month as soon as they
come off the presses. I understand that I will be billed only $2.25
for each book (total $9.00). There are no shipping or handling
charges. There is no minimum number of books that I have to
purchase. In fact, I may cancel this arrangement at any time.
Twice in a Lifetime is mine to keep as a FREE gift, even if I do not
buy any additional books.

Name _____ (please print)

Address _____ Apt. no. _____

City _____ State/Prov. _____ Zip/Postal Code _____

Signature (If under 18, parent or guardian must sign.)